MARIE-HÉLÈNE LEBEAULT
AUTHOR OF THE EVERS SERIES

UTOPIA

A WHAT HAPPENS NEXT NOVEL

First published by Beaches and Trails Publishing 2024
Copyright © 2024 by Marie-Hélène Lebeault
All rights reserved.

Editing by Jessica McKenna
Proofreading by Hilde Pols
Cover by Marie-Hélène Lebeault

BEACHES AND TRAILS
PUBLISHING

ABOUT THE AUTHOR

Positive, uplifting books and stories.

Marie-Hélène is a Canadian author. She writes young adult quest and adventure stories rooted fantasy, magic, space and time travel. With important coming-of-age lessons at the core of her writing, readers will revel in the fantastical journeys of her characters.

When not immersed magic and mystery, you'll find Marie-Hélène hiking, cycling, or lying on the beach with a good book. A retired teacher, she lives in Quebec, Canada with her grown children.

Website Email Newsletter

facebook.com/mhlebeaultauthor

x.com/mhlebeault

instagram.com/mhlebeault

amazon.com/author/mhlebeault

bookbub.com/authors/marie-helene-lebeault

goodreads.com/mhlebeault

linkedin.com/in/mhlebeault

tiktok.com/@mhlebeaultauthor

youtube.com/@mhlebeault

ALSO BY MARIE-HÉLÈNE LEBEAULT

PROLOGUE: FROM DARKNESS TO DAWN

Mama and Dada are crying.

Lindsey holds her parents' hands in the crush of people as they slowly move forward. It started way back hours ago. Lindsey chews her lips and pouts, but the tears that Mama and Dada keep wiping away make her scared.

Adults aren't supposed to cry. Lindsey wants to shout at them, to tell them it's not fair that they're crying. She is the one that doesn't get a birthday anymore. She's turning five, and she was promised that they would go to Disney Land.

This isn't Disneyland. She knows it isn't. Where's Mickey Mouse? Where's Goofy? Nobody is here except people. So many people are all in a line.

Sometimes, the men in black uniforms lead people away. These people are sobbing and screaming. Whenever they come by, Mama puts her hands over Lindsey's ears.

Lindsey hates all of this.

"I want to go to Disney Land," she says, stomping her foot. Maybe if she starts to sob and scream, the black uniforms will come to take her and her parents out of this line. Then they can go to Disneyland. "I don't want to be here!"

"Peter, we have to tell her," Mama says.

Peter is Mama's name for Dada. Lindsey has different names, too. Names like Honey and Sweetheart. Grandpa calls her Little Miss Sunshine.

"Where is Grandpa?" Lindsey asks, trying to pull her hand away from Dada. "It's my birthday. Where is Grandpa?"

Dada picks Lindsey up. "Stop."

"Where's Grandpa?" Lindsey shrieks, her voice growing louder. "Where?"

"Peter," Mama says.

Dada's arms are so tight around Lindsay that it hurts. She twists and turns but can't get herself free. She starts to cry, but Mama tells her to be quiet.

"Do you want to be left behind?" Mama asks.

She sounds so frightened it makes Lindsey's tummy hurt. She stops fighting. Tears run down her face, but she tries not to cry.

Mama looks away.

"We're going to a new home," Dada says. "A beautiful home. We're going to be happy. I promise."

Lindsey thinks they're already happy, but she can't say anything anymore.

They get to the front of the line, and Dada hands the man three pieces of paper. The man's hard eyes sweep over them, and then he tells them to go to an elevator.

Lindsey used to like elevators.

It's dark and cold inside. It makes her shiver, but she knows she's not allowed to fight anymore. She clings around Dada's neck as the doors close.

"Why are we here?" she finally asks.

The doors open again. Dada carries her out of the elevator and looks around. They pass through long hallways that are filled with bunk beds up and down every side.

Lindsey likes bunk beds, but even though lights are running

down the ceiling, it's dark here. There aren't any windows. It makes her feel like she might throw up.

"Here we are," Mama says when they get to a bunk bed that looks like all the other ones. There are three drawers underneath it, and Mama pulls open one to reveal folded clothes. She sighs as she pulls out a sheet. "Help me get this up around it."

Dada puts Lindsey down.

She watches Mama and Dada put up the curtain, and then they take Lindsey into the small area in the low bunk that's been hidden away.

"I want to go home," Lindsey says.

Dada kisses her forehead. "This is our home now, Honey. You see, there's something bad happening. Some people were digging in the Arctic, and they hit something they shouldn't have. A big, poisonous ball of gas was released."

"Lots of smart people are working to fix it," Mama says. "But right now, we have to be down here. Clever machines are cleaning the air for us. We just have to wait until it's no longer poisonous."

Lindsey shivers. "What about Grandpa?"

Dada and Mama look at each other.

"There are lots and lots of places like this," Mama says. "Under the ground and under the sea. Everywhere that the poison can't get. Grandpa is going to a different place. There wasn't any more room here."

Lindsey leans against Mama, her stomach hurting even more.

It's the first time she ever realized that parents can lie to you.

The graduation room is filled with plants. Plants with broad leaves, plants with bright flowers, plants offering bounteous fruit.

It's all proof of how well the students have done this year.

Lindsey stands tall with the rest of her class. She's fortunate that she was accepted into the climate restoration program, and now at eighteen, she's the youngest to graduate. After thirteen long years of living in the fallout shelter, she has come to understand far better what drove them down here in the first place.

Mom and Dad sit in the front row, both smiling proudly at her.

Elder Thomas, the leader of Shelter Forty-Three A, nicknamed FAST because of the recent food shortage crisis, smiles at the fresh graduates.

"You will be assigned duties with the restoration crews immediately," he says. "If you wish to pursue further education to join the terraforming engineers, you may apply in six months. We are so proud of all of you."

"Thank you, Elder," everyone answers, bowing.

Elder Thomas claps his hands. "Now, let's celebrate this auspicious occasion!"

Music is put on, and the parents get up and come forward to congratulate their children.

"We're so proud of you," Dad says, hugging Lindsey. "You've worked hard and proved yourself."

Lindsey smiles back at him. "I couldn't have done it without you."

It's true. Dad was given a spot in the shelter because he was an engineer even before the Fallout. Lindsey was given a spot because she was his daughter.

Mom had to buy her way in. It took all of their money... and Grandpa's money.

Thirteen years later, Lindsey prays her thanks to her grandfather every night.

Lindsey hugs her parents again and moves to dance with her friends. It's a night of celebration, after all.

The latest reports show that the air pollution above the surface has been scrubbed down a full two percent since the terraforming project was started ten years ago. With all these new students and improved technology, they will get this going even faster.

Projections currently estimate that the land above will be habitable again in three hundred years; once the air is cleared the atmosphere will have to be restored and that will take the longest time.

Lindsey hopes one day, she will have distant grandchildren who will walk under the sun once more.

"We have the protective suits. I just think we should be allowed to go to the surface to get more accurate readings," Paula argues.

Lindsey is on her lunch break with a handful of her friends. Rumors circulate that the planet's atmosphere hasn't been as damaged as first feared. It's possible that the cloud was so dense it stayed within the troposphere.

"It was a hoax," Bel answers, scratching his clean-shaven chin. "There's no evidence that the stratosphere colonies survived the event. Even if they did—"

"We have evidence in the message," Paula interrupts.

Lindsey puts her hands up, sighing. "Stop it, both of you. I get your point, Bel, but if we take the proper precautions and test the airlocks thoroughly, the risk of the cloud getting in is minimal. We need to set up new air scrubbers, anyway. Cleaning production has dropped off almost twenty percent over the last year."

Bel rubs the back of his neck, looking unconvinced.

"Something needs to change," Lindsey says, her gaze growing grim as she stares at the nutrient blocks on her plate. Her only rations for the day. "People are growing restless."

Too much has changed over the last five years.

Lindsey sits in the Prime Councilor's seat, uncomfortable, yet determined to make the most of this chance.

There's only so much that people can take when they're starving. As the Elder Council grew weaker and weaker, the younger people made a change. It wasn't easy, and there were unfortunate instances where talking devolved into violence.

It's over now, though. The Elders have all stepped aside, some more willing than others.

The first act Lindsey passed as Prime Councilor was to send people to the surface. Repair teams for the terraforming machines. Research teams to test the ground and the air, and see exactly how far the cloud went.

And now they are all returning. Lindsey's stomach tightens with nerves. Her fellow council members sit with her in a long line at the front of the room as the teams stream in.

"Paula Vonn," Lindsey calls on her old colleague. "What did you find?"

Paula strides forward with purpose, her eyes shining as she does so. A smile breaks over her face.

"The cloud never reached the stratosphere, Councilor," Paula announces. "The floating cities may have survived after all. We could not make contact as of yet but have set up a radio relay system that we can monitor for any further communication."

Lindsey leans forward. "This is excellent news. Perhaps the damage to the world wasn't as bad as we first feared."

The team leader for the scrubber repairs, Johann, steps forward now. "On this news, I'm afraid we have bad news. The scrubbers that were installed above the surface have completely degraded. The amount of acid rain caused by the cloud was greater than the original estimates. Nothing could be saved. We'll have to build entirely new scrubbers."

Lindsey nods, though this information weighs heavily. It's not good to know that all of that has to be replaced. Where will they get the raw materials?

"And how can we prevent the new scrubbers from being damaged the same way?" another council member asks.

Johann sighs and shakes his head. "We're not sure yet. We brought back samples to run diagnostics on. The soil itself is highly acidic, so we will have to develop something that lifts the scrubbers and shields them from the rain."

"Before that can be developed, we need to know the strength of the acid," Lindsey murmurs.

This is a setback she isn't prepared for. If her parents were still here, what would they suggest?

She wishes desperately that she had her father's engineering knowledge to fall back on now.

"How long before the diagnostics are complete?" she asks.

Johann straightens. "We started running them as soon as we got back. I'll have a report to you within the week."

"Thank you," Lindsey says.

She folds her hands over the table as she listens to the rest of the reports. Some vegetation has survived, but so far there has been no sign of animal life, other than a few species of insects.

When the reports are done, she stands.

"You have gathered important knowledge," she tells the teams. "Thank you. Soon we'll be able to implement the terraforming technology above the surface to cleanse it from the disaster. We will return to the sun in our lifetime. We will build a new world, safe and plentiful, for our children."

They owed it to the next generation, who had never known life above the surface.

Lindsey takes a deep breath, quelling her nausea. She can't imagine what their lives will be like if they are forced to stay in this dark world where everything is constantly in short supply.

Lindsey's heart hammers as she holds her daughter's hand. The old elevators broke down long ago, their parts scavenged, and so it's been a four-day journey walking up the shafts dug to allow the population of FAST to leave their underground home.

Megan whines, pulling at Lindsey's hand. "Mama, I'm tired!"

"I know, Little Miss Sunshine," Lindsey says. She picks Megan up and strokes her hair. "It's been twenty-five years. We thought it was going to take three hundred or more years, but it was only twenty-five years."

Her legs are tired, too, from the constant upward climb.

The air feels different.

And when the first sign of light comes from above her, tears stream down her face. She can only imagine the feelings that her parents must have had as they went down to the Earth that day.

Now she's coming out of it. Full of hopes and prayers that this will be enough. That she is making the right choice.

They emerge into a world that looks nothing like the one Lindsey remembers.

The desolation the cloud left behind is worse than any of Lindsey's nightmares. The once-thriving city of Vancouver had been on this very spot. Now, the buildings have broken and collapsed. Remnants of skyscrapers twist into grotesque shapes, their steel frames melted by the acid rains.

What was once green and lush with ferns and trees is a barren gray. The sun blazes fiercely overhead, as strong as the most unforgiving desert. The ground is baked dry. Not even the most hardy of plants have been able to take root here. Harsh winds whip across the dead city, bringing with it the scent of dust and death.

The silence is broken by Megan's whimpers. "I want to go home."

Beside her, Bel sighs. He's a recently elected member of the council and was opposed to leaving the fallout shelter so early.

"It will take a lot of work to restore it," he says. "I don't think we can salvage anything from the city."

Lindsey nods once. "Then we won't salvage it. We let go of the past and rebuild. Someday we might build over this place but for now, we will start closer to the mountains. New Vancouver will rise. It will be the home we need it to be."

Bel looks doubtful.

"We can't stay below," Lindsey tells him. "We don't have the supplies. We need this land. We need to collect new resources. Grow new food."

"If anything can grow at all," Bel says.

Megan whimpers.

Lindsey smooths her hair and kisses her forehead. "This is our home now. And look." She points at the sky. "That's the sun. We're back to where we belong."

Lindsey sits in her wheelchair, looking out the window. Her hands are laid in her lap. The constant ache of her arthritis isn't as bad today as usual.

She sighs as her granddaughter, Sylvia, steps up to the chair and starts pushing it.

"It's been eighty years since we left the fallout shelter," she says. "I was only thirty then."

"I know, Grandma," Sylvia replies.

She has just been elected to the Elder Council. Sixty-two years old. A grandmother herself. Lindsey hums. She never believed she would one day be one hundred and ten years old, and yet here she is.

Her eyes might not see as well as they once did, but when Sylvia wheels her into the council chambers, she can still see the three teenagers standing in the middle of the room.

"Eldest Lindsey," one of them says, bowing to her. "We have come with a plea. Let go of the past and embrace the future. Otherwise, everything will have been in vain."

RYN'S JOURNEY

THEY SAY THAT LONG AGO, before the oceans froze over, you could see the stars—bright pinpricks of light that scattered as far as the eye could see, too many to count. But that's just a myth, a legend the Elders tell the children, like so many other tales from the past.

Now we live in the ocean's deep. No one ventures up to the ice barrier because it protects us from the deadly smog that permeates the air on land. So we remain in the safety of the Dome, miles below the ice.

Everyone has developed gills or has found a way to breathe underwater - everyone but me. I'm the last unaltered human, despite being born and raised in the Dome.

I used to go swimming with the others. But since they started regulating air consumption, I'm no longer allowed to use the suits. So now I spend all of my time in the Dome, making myself useful.

Today I'm helping to clean the air scrubbers. Irta came down with a cold, and I'm filling in for her. Our group spends the first part of the day cleaning the inside scrubbers before the others head outside to clean the pumps. I watch them leave before heading to the park to meet up with my friend, Aalton. We've stuck together for as long as either of us can remember. Like most Aquatics, Aalton has gills on his neck, but he's also grown a set of bright pink scales on his arms and legs. They're supposed to help him swim faster, but he's still the slowest in our class. Even I can outpace him.

I arrive at the park to discover that a large group has assembled at the center podium. Looking around, I spot Aalton and jog over to him. He has a look of concern on his face, and the gills on his neck flare as he stares intently at the group around the podium. He's not wearing his usual attire. Instead, he's wearing the standard blue slip-stream that all Aquatics wear when they're about to head out into the ocean.

A slip-stream is a special suit made of algae and minerals harvested outside the Dome, allowing the wearer to travel through water with less resistance. Most of them are blue; the Elders have special golden ones that stand out.

"Hey, Aalton!" I give him a wave. "What's going on?"

Aalton turns towards me, flashing a smile that doesn't reach his eyes. "Hey, Ryn," he says softly.

Something isn't right.

"Aalton," I say, cupping his face towards me. "What aren't you telling me?"

He stares down at his feet, pondering silently for a drawn-out moment.

"The Dome is failing. The maintenance crew has been running tests. They don't think the Dome will last for more than a few days."

I freeze, my hand still on his face, almost petrified. It can't be.

"You can't be serious." I can barely get the words out. "That's impossible. The Dome is fully operational."

He doesn't argue or joke. He just stares at me with sadness in his eyes. We both know that I'm the only one whose life depends on the Dome.

Dread spreads through my gut.

If the Dome fails, I will die.

Looking around, I realize that I've taken several steps back. I shake like a scared animal about to flee. Everything blurs as I hear Elder Valdimar speak behind me.

"We only have seventy-two hours of oxygen left. We need to travel to Aquata." I turn to see him looking at me. His eyes are wet. "We've known for some time that this would happen. But fear not: the new city will support all of us."

Deafening silence falls.

"All except for one."

I feel nauseous, angry, and abandoned. I flee.

The Dome is enormous, but suddenly feels suffocating. I run to where the scrubbers are working. How could they fail us?

Irta is with the scrubbers, her skin still a little pale from being sick. One of their external panels is on the ground next to her toolbox. She looks as if she is trying to find out what's wrong with it - or destroy it. I'm too far away to tell which.

"Irta!" I shout to her.

She turns around and waves her wrench at me, beckoning me over.

"Judging from the look on your face, I'm assuming you heard the news?" she calmly asks as I stop next to her.

"Yeah." I stare down at the open panel. "Are you trying to fix it?"

"No. The panels can't be fixed." Irta points at a couple of wires inside the scrubber. "They haven't worked in years. The only reason there is even still air in the Dome is because of the park. But the trees can't produce enough oxygen to sustain the entire place."

I lean forward and look at the wires. They have burn marks and signs of water damage. Looking closer, I notice how the scrubber itself seems broken. Screws and bolts are missing. The gears are worn, and the fan blades are bent at odd angles.

"Why hasn't anybody tried to fix these yet?" I ask, poking a finger at it.

"We can't," Irta says softly, nodding towards her toolbox. "These are the last of the supplies that were brought from land. Even if we had the tools to fix the scrubbers, the Elders would have us work on other Dome systems, like the power supply."

Grimacing, I think about the recent spike in power failures. Even if the scrubbers were working, there would be no telling for how much longer. Something was constantly breaking. Maybe the pumps would stop working, or the water purifiers would malfunction.

"Then why do we clean the scrubbers every day if they've been broken for years?" I ask Irta with increasing frustration.

"The Elders did not wish to reveal just how close to failing the Dome was. They've known this day was coming for decades. Why else do you think they've been building a fully functional underwater city?" She laughs without humor before continuing. "They've been planning this ever since the first scrubber showed signs of wear. They would've had us leave the Dome already, but then you were born. They couldn't just leave you here. So they stalled, but now our time is up."

Irta pulls a small box out of the scrubber and disconnects it. Suddenly, their low humming ceases plunging the entire Dome into silence. She turns towards me, holding up the box in her hands.

"They installed these after the last scrubber failed," she explains. "They're meant to keep up the illusion that they actually work." She drops the device in her toolbox. "I only found out today when they asked me to remove it. No sense in wasting any more power on it." She finishes packing up and turns towards me. "Listen, Ryn. I know you're worried. I would be, too, if I were you. If the Elders pull off the relocation in time, you'll have years' worth of oxygen."

"And if they don't?" I ask, eyes boring into hers.

She looks away. "We can only hope. It's all we have to count on." The sentence hangs between us, and Irta walks away.

I'm still standing by the now silent scrubbers, wiping tears from my cheeks, when Elder Valdimar finds me. He silently hands me a piece of candy and beckons me to sit down next to him. I pop the sweet in my mouth, waiting for him to explain why he's here. Like the other Elders, Valdimar appears almost perfectly human. A small set of gills peek out above his slip-stream. As the head Elder, Valdimar has a unique silver slip-stream, which he rarely wears.

If there is a day to wear it, it's today.

"Ryn," he finally says. "I know that this comes as a shock. Believe me. We wanted to tell you sooner. We really did. But Aquata wasn't ready yet. It still isn't, but if we put off the relocation any longer, the oxygen levels will drop below the point of no return. We need to leave. The Dome is your home. It can support a handful of occupants for decades so that you won't be entirely alone."

His eyes travel to the edge of the Dome, where a line of Aquatics are preparing to leave for the new city—a place I'll never get to see.

We sit quietly, watching the exodus. It will take a few days to move everyone.

"Why?" I ask Valdimar. I cringe at how whiny I sound. "Why go through all this trouble for me?"

"Follow me," he says, rising from his spot on the ground. "I'll show you why we're doing this."

I get up to follow him.

He leads me through the city, down roads and paths I've walked a thousand times. Heading to the Citadel in the center of the Dome, he nods at the guards stationed at the gate. We are immediately granted access. Valdimar guides us into the heart of the city, past the Elders' quarters, beyond the meeting rooms, and below the prison cells, deep underground. We reached a dead-end.

Elder Valdimar places a hand on the stone wall, moving it slowly until a panel opens up. Reaching in, he pulls out a scroll.

"Open it," he says gently, handing it to me.

Gingerly, I take it. The paper feels ancient, almost as if it might disintegrate. I unroll it slowly, and am stunned at what I see.

It's a painting—of me. With a glint in my eye, my face is a mix of awe and determination. I'm standing on the ice barrier, surrounded by what can only be described as lightning bolts. The ice beneath my feet is cracked and broken from where the lightning struck, but I appear unharmed.

"We discovered the painting a few days before you were born. Our initial interpretation was that it was a mysterious artifact, something from the old world. But as years went by and the older you grew, the more you resembled the figure in the painting. We knew you had to be special and have been trying to buy you extra time. Whatever this painting is, it's clearly a clue to your destiny."

"Who found it?" I ask, awestruck.

Valdimar is silent for a moment. "I did. I was exploring the caves when I stumbled upon this dead-end. Exhausted, I leaned a hand against the wall, only to have the rocks slide inwards. Afraid of falling into another hollow, I snatched my hand away and stepped back. You can only imagine my amazement when the stone slid back into place. I figured there was a secret passage of some sort and started pressing the stones in a distinct pattern. It took a while, but eventually, that panel opened. I pulled out the scroll and showed the painting to the other Elders. We had a copy made and put the original back down here."

"So ..." I say slowly, considering it, "you found the scroll, but you do not know who painted it?"

Valdimar shakes his head. "If I knew, I would have told you."

I hide my disappointment, having silently hoped in those long minutes that one of my parents would be revealed as the painter. Both had perished on one of the work ships weeks after I was born.

"Okay. So what now?"

"I need to check on the progress of the move and make sure everything is going according to plan," he answers, beginning to lead the way out of the caves.

In the hallway, my toe catches on a rock, and I tumble to the ground. Dust rains from the ceiling from the impact, and I quickly get back to my feet and continue. In the stairway, Elder Valdimar notices a fallen painting. We glance at each other uneasily. My fall should not have dislodged the painting. We climb the stairs two at a time, the sound of our feet echoing as we round the last corner. Padding down the narrow path in Valdimar's wake, I notice that other items have fallen off the shelves in the meeting rooms. As we near the guards, one of them heads us off.

"Sir," he says briskly, a slight tremor in his voice. "They need you at the north gate. There's been a fight." The guard pauses, his eyes flickering to me. "And sir... they've damaged the Dome."

The guard barely finishes delivering his message before Valdimar is off like a shot, bolting down the street faster than a man his age should be able to. The guard and I follow suit. I glimpse the Dome as we rush out of the Citadel. There are massive cracks in it, visible even from here. The damage is not the result of a mere disagreement. Even as I run, I can hear water flowing through the cracks. A team of Aquatics is trying to stop the fractures from spreading. They can't seem to figure out why the pumps aren't working as the ocean pours into the Dome.

By the time I've caught up to Valdimar, the water has already risen substantially. The Dome encases a small underwater mountain; the four gates are positioned at the mountain's base for this exact reason. Valdimar stands at the edge of the water, calmly giving orders in a semi-successful attempt to manage the chaos. I watch as he sends Aquatics to fetch the sealant while others are tasked with starting the backup pumps. A team of guards is dispatched to the other gates for added security as citizens are rerouted.

Valdimar's voice is loud and firm yet reassuring as he guides the crowd away from the north gate. As the last of them clears the area, the water has finally slowed its ascension. This part of the Dome is flooded, and the water creeps higher up my legs.

HOURS AFTER THE INCIDENT, they still have not fixed the pumps, and we run out of sealant. The backup pumps cannot drain the water, but they keep it at a steady level. It turns out the Dome was damaged when an angry citizen smashed a nearby fuel tank after a heated encounter with a guard. The rupture caused a mini explosion, killing both the guard and the citizen in the process. Several Aquatics are injured and have to be treated before they can leave. The delay has ruined any hope I might have had of living in the Dome. While the sealant slows the flooding, the cracks are spreading. The engineers openly estimate that the pumps will fail in the next twenty-four hours. Water floods parks and fields. The food supply is shot. The handful of taller trees is not nearly enough to sustain even a single citizen. Every passerby averts their gaze from me as they head to the nearest gate. They know I'm dead in the water - pun intended.

I decide to spend my final hours in the small park facing the Citadel. I'm looking at the painting when Aalton rounds a corner. I wave him over, and we chat about the new city, skimming over the poignant fact that I will not be joining the others.

"What do you think the city will look like?" Aalton asks.

I shrug.

"I bet it's made of candy," he muses, staring off into space.

"Nah, it's going to be made of gold," I joke.

It quickly becomes a game of who can come up with the most ridiculous description. I win as I describe a city made of diamonds atop a massive turtle with rock candy for scales. Laughing, Aalton concedes the victory to me and gets up to leave. I get up as well. It's time for him to go.

"Aalton..." I begin hesitantly, "there's something I need to show you."

I pull out the scroll and hand it to him. He unfurls it and cocks his head.

"Who painted this?" he asks, confused. "And why are you being struck by lightning?"

"I have no idea. Elder Valdimar found this a few days before I was born."

"Wait, what? How can it have been painted before you were born?"

I shrug. Aalton observes the painting, then me. "Where is the smog?"

At my blank expression, he adds, "Isn't the surface covered with a deadly layer of brown gasses?"

"It is, isn't it?" I answer, nodding my head.

"That's what we've been told. Perhaps this is a prophecy!" He points to the scroll still in his hands, his eyes sparkling with new hope. "Maybe the painter didn't include the smog because it's cleared up, and the air is now pure. Maybe you could actually live up there!" He nearly shouts the last sentence excitedly.

I see where he is going with this. His enthusiasm is contagious, but hope feels like too much of an indulgence. I take the scroll from him and study the image.

"It could be a warning," I say. "Travel to the surface, and you'll be struck by lightning."

"True, but who looks that happy while being struck by lightning?" Aalton counters. "It might be a symbol of triumph." He grabs the scroll back from me. "Either way, what do you have to lose? If you stay, you'll die. If you go, there's a chance you could make it."

I nod grimly before realizing something. "How am I supposed to get to the surface? I can't breathe underwater, remember?"

He frowns, thinking. None of our ships are outfitted for air-breathing humans, only Aquatics. If I tried to take one, I'd drown long before reaching the surface.

"Maybe Elder Valdimar has a ship," Aalton finally suggests, clearly less confident than he was a moment ago. "If anyone has a ship you can use, it'll be him."

He turns to look towards the southern gate. It's time for him to go.

We exchange a quick hug before walking down the stairs together. I wave goodbye and head to find Elder Valdimar. I check with the guards, and they inform me he's overseeing the line of Aquatics exiting through the south gate. If I'd known, I'd have walked with Aalton.

I find Valdimar talking with another Elder.

"Elder Jauhar," I address him, "may I have a word with Elder Valdimar?" She nods, stepping aside to allow me to speak with him privately.

"How can I help you, Ryn?" he asks.

"Aalton thinks the scroll is predicting that I will find a way through the barrier," I whisper near his ear, not wanting anyone else to overhear. "The only problem is that I need a ship."

Valdimar purses his lips. "I'm afraid the last of the human vessels broke over a decade ago." He glances up to where the cracks are spreading. They have nearly reached the top of the Dome, and it looks like the entire north side is ready to collapse. "If I remember correctly, the barrier is ten miles beyond the Dome. Even in our fastest ships, you'd suffocate long before reaching the top." He looks down to where the last of the Aquatics are waiting by the gate. "However," Valdimar pauses as a hush spreads around them. The backup pumps have died. Turning back to me, he continues, "there is a device called a rebreather. It allows one to breathe underwater without a suit for about 90 minutes, which should be enough to get you to the surface."

"Great! Where can I get one?" I ask, hardly able to contain my excitement.

"Unfortunately, the last working rebreather was in the depot next to the north gate..." he trails off.

I sigh, defeated. I know what Elder Valdimar is implying: only an Aquatic can retrieve it now that the northern gate is underwater. I thank him when he holds up a hand, a sly smile beginning to form on his lips.

"Luckily for you, Aalton asked about it a few minutes before you arrived. Provided nothing has gone wrong, he should be returning with it right about ... now."

Aalton runs up to us, panting and brandishing a strange device. He beams with excitement as he hands it to Valdimar. "I found it!" he shouts excitedly. "It was right where you said it would be, sir. It has a few dents and some rust, but should work fine."

Elder Valdimar checks the device. There is hope in Aalton's eyes, hope that his best friend will live. Deeming it functional, the Elder hands me the device and briefly explains how it works. It's pretty simple.

Once I've got the hang of it, he beckons Elder Jauhar who leads me to the ship. It's a small, sleek craft designed for speed and maneuverability. After showing me how to pilot it, Jauhar wishes me safe travels and leaves.

I look around. Everyone is gone but the three of us. It's time to say goodbye.

"Thank you, Elder Valdimar." I give him a half bow. "I shall never forget you."

"Nor I, you," he replies, placing a hand on my shoulder.

I turn to Aalton and give him one last hug. "Thank you, Aalton."

He hugs me back before gesturing towards the ship. "Thank us once you breach the barrier."

As they head for the gate, I go towards the ship. I have to crawl to enter the cockpit, but it is long enough to stretch out comfortably once inside. I close the hatch and fasten the rebreather. Once it is in place, I flood the compartment, and the craft sinks beneath the waves. Steering it towards the gate, I crank the jets and shoot out of the Dome.

I drive as fast as I can, dodging fish and aquatic flora. I've never traveled this fast - it's invigorating. I turn to look at the gate and see Aalton and Valdimar, now mere dots, as they head to their new home.

The Dome silently collapses, and I turn to face my future.

THE DOME'S collapse has given the ship a bit of a push, and soon I can see the ice. I hover under it, checking for cracks or a spot that might yield more easily.

After what feels like hours, I still haven't found a passage through. Hope is dwindling as fast as the time I have left. The rebreather is running out of air; my breaths are shallow, and I feel dizzy. I ram the ice with the ship, but it barely scratches it. Backing up the craft, I toggle the jets to the max, and the ship vaults towards the ice at a breakneck speed. If this fails, there will be no second attempt.

The barrier creeps closer as the ship gains momentum. A flash of light temporarily blinds me as the hull hits the ice. For a minute, I think I haven't breached the barrier. Everything is dark.

I hear cracking. Is it the ship? The ice? The ship tilts to the right. I hang on tight as it flips over, rising slowly and then bobbing up on the surface.

I made it.

I wiggle out of the cockpit and open the hatch. I'm floating in the middle of a cracked patch of ice, the water quickly freezing over and trapping the ship. The air isn't as cold as the water, but it's still chilly. My insulated suit has kept me dry. Hopefully, it will keep me warm. I grab my backpack and any supplies within arm's reach. It's time to abandon the ship.

As I step onto the surface, I marvel at the vapor my breath makes and at the crunching sound of my boots on the ice. It's dark, but there is enough moonlight to make my way toward the shore. That's when I look up and see them—millions upon millions of stars. It's the most beautiful thing I've ever seen: it takes my breath away. None of the etchings I've been shown throughout my life have captured the infinite beauty that is before me. As I stand under the night sky, I don't feel so alone.

I press on. I finally reach the shore and scan the horizon. I spot some odd-looking bushes and decide they will provide adequate shelter and protect me from the elements for now. I lay down and use my bag as a pillow.

Tomorrow I will explore this new land. Tonight, I sleep under the stars.

2

EIRA'S JOURNEY

MY LUNGS ARE BURNING.

I keep my eyes closed, afraid that if I open them, the world will continue to spin. The coolness of the floor beneath me and the ice packs around my body help with the nausea, but who knows how long it will last? Every inch of my body aches.

The medication that flows through me isn't enough to hold off the pain. This is the worst one yet... although I suppose every time I wake up from surgery, I think the same thing.

There's a soft breeze right around my mouth and nose. I know from its presence that I'm not breathing on my own. At least I'm not intubated this time. My lungs work, pulling in air, and releasing it. I just need a higher percentage of oxygen than exists up here in the stratosphere.

As I come back to myself, the intensity of the pain lessens. I'm able to feel out with my senses with everything else around me. The sound of the heartbeat monitor, the iciness of the packs around me— meant to lower metabolism and prevent brain damage during the surgery—the still-bitter dryness in my mouth from the medications.

Another failure. Every procedure I've undergone helps me adapt to the environment here in Fata Morgana, where I and the rest of the

Aerians live. The city was named for a phenomenon that, through an optical illusion, made it look like there was a city floating in the sky.

Now, there is. This place.

Everyone here has adapted to the thin atmosphere to varying degrees. Everyone except me.

I hear voices over the hum of the equipment and strain my ears. It soon becomes clear it's my parents and Doctor Heather, the surgeon who has been working with me since I was a baby.

"What are our next steps?" Dad asks, his tone strained.

Doctor Heather sighs. "I'm afraid there isn't much we can do. Eira simply can't adapt. We can keep putting her through these procedures, but unfortunately, they simply won't work. We're out of options. There is nothing to be done."

Mom snaps back, "So we should just let her die, then?"

My heart rate spikes, measured by the beeps, but I take deep breaths, pushing aside the pain to do so.

Die. I've known since the time I was little that one day I'd die. My body can't handle the atmosphere. It's not just the oxygen, but the sun's intensity. I'm not built for this.

I don't want any more procedures, though. I'm tired of it.

But I don't want to die.

There has to be something else.

Fingers comb through my hair. Mom. I pretend to still be sleeping. I can't stand to look at the pain in her eyes.

I'm in the hospital for a week longer than usual, so when I can go back home, it's a relief.

Well... 'home' might be the wrong word for it. There's a group home for people who, like me, have trouble with the adaptations. It's specially designed to have a higher oxygen concentration and a thicker construction to shield it from the sun.

There are people of all ages here. Most of them will only stay for a week or two in recovery after a procedure. A few unlucky folks will end up here for a few months. Other than me, the longest-term resident was one of the Elders, who had been one of the first people to have the adaptations done to them.

Those adaptations from the early days were failing the Elder. They were too old to undergo more procedures and lived here for an entire year before they passed peacefully in their sleep.

It's selfish to wish for someone else to live here as long as me, and so I try not to. It gets lonely, though, when I only have visitors or workers to make friends with. A few of the others who stayed here have come back to visit me from time to time.

It's a busy life up here above the clouds, though, and I understand it's not always possible for people to come see me.

"Eira," one of the workers, Daisy Mae, comes over to me as I sit in the window. "I'm getting some strange reading from your breathing apparatus. Can I check it quick?"

I nod and she kneels next to me, fiddling with the tank that I have to bring everywhere with me.

Even here, in this place that's specially developed for those with weak lungs, I have to have extra help. The tank is specially designed to filter the air and collect a higher concentration of oxygen for me. My face is constantly breaking out from having to wear the mask.

"It looks alright," Daisy Mae says as she straightens. "Are you feeling okay? Any dizziness?"

"No, I'm fine," I tell her. "I was just admiring the beauty outside."

I nod at the window. Sunlight gleams off the rows of white buildings beneath us, almost blinding. Tall, twisting trees cast shade here and there. It looks beautiful, like something out of a dream. Sometimes I can't understand how lucky I have to be to see this every day.

Daisy Mae pats my shoulder. "Looks like you're due to have a visit by your sister soon. Are you excited?"

I nod, smiling. It's always nice when my family stops by.

I take some more time at the window, enjoying the view, before the city's rotation shifts in such a way that the sunlight comes directly at me.

At this point, I retreat to my room. It was specially designed, too, after it became apparent I would never adapt enough to leave the group home. So, it's bigger than all the other rooms. In fact, there were originally three of them, but the walls were taken down so I could have more space. I spent weeks painting the mural along the east wall. It's a beautiful forest filled with butterflies and small birds, like the old films show.

My bed sits in the corner, away from the windows, and thick blinds can come down and block out the sun entirely. The carpet is soft and cozy, and I have shelves on shelves on shelves of books. I love books more than anything else in the world. I have them arranged in a rainbow, and I know where each one is.

Elzi, my oldest sister, comes to see me a little bit after I've gone to my room. She smiles at me. We look alike, with straight black hair, and large, inky-blue eyes. I'm shorter and thinner than she is. Anyone who looks at us thinks I'm her daughter rather than her sister. But then, they also usually think I'm closer to twelve than sixteen.

"How are you doing?" she asks me as we sit at a little table.

"I'm doing alright," I tell her, going to my small kitchenette to put some water on for tea. "I've been having dreams about the old days again. This time, I was running through a wheat field. It's probably because I watched a prairie documentary before I went to sleep last night."

I laugh as I arrange ginger, peppercorn, and black tea leaves in a strainer. I love making tea. It always helps me calm down.

Once it's ready, I serve it and take a seat again. Here in my room, I have the option of increasing the oxygen flow, but for it to be comfortable for me, it would make Elzi sick. So, instead, we have a compromise where neither of us feels quite right.

"What's new with you?" I ask her.

She smiles, but it looks sad. "I'm pregnant."

In an instant, I know what this means. I don't care. I just clap my hands and squeal in delight. "Oh, that's so exciting! When are you due?"

"In December."

Elzi's smile grows even more sad. "Eira, it means I won't have as much extra money to send to you anymore."

I wave a hand. "The Elders provide everything I need. Nobody goes without, and I'll adjust to it. Maybe it'll even encourage me to write that book, huh? Then I'll sell it and have so much money I'll be sending some for you."

Elzi hugs me. "You're the best, you know that?"

"Of course I do," I tease. "You tell me I'm the best too often for me to forget."

I wink at her.

We talk for some time, and I make sure to focus on the happy things. A new baby is something that should be celebrated. Oh, sure, I won't get as many extras, but I have food, a safe place to live, and everything I need. I'll be just fine, and Elzi shouldn't feel guilty for living her life.

I try my best not to be a burden on the city or my family. The Council decreed long ago that every citizen would have their needs met. I know I'm expensive, with all this extra stuff that I've needed just so that I can breathe. It's not right for my sisters to feel that burden.

I'm fine. I'm happy. Sure, I wish for things I can't have, but who doesn't? I am surrounded by beautiful things and people who care for me.

What else can a girl ask for?

THE NEXT MORNING, my parents come to see me. They're all smiles, but I see how strained they are. I can tell by the lingering odor of the hospital on them they had been to see the doctor. I wonder what questions they asked this time and if the answers were all the same.

There doesn't seem to be a reason for the adaptations to fail. It's not genetic. There's nothing my parents could have done differently.

Sometimes these things just happen. No, it's never happened in the history of Fata Morgana, but also consider that we haven't been here for long in the grand scheme of things. Only one hundred and five years. That's not a long time.

I'm the first. I won't be the last. The research done on my condition will help generations to come. With any luck, I'll be the key to figuring out what went wrong, and people in the future won't suffer my same fate.

As bleak as it is, there is some comfort in knowing that I might provide answers for the future.

"Hey, Sweetheart," Dad greets me, kissing my temple.

Mom smiles as she sinks onto the couch next to me. Little by little, these last few years, she's stopped calling me 'sweetheart.' Most times, she's fighting not to cry. Dad can hide that better than she is.

It's just one thing that make them different. Dad is better at living in the present, while Mom is always looking into the future. It's what makes them work so well together as a couple. They complement each other.

I'm not sure I ever wanted to have a marriage. Sometimes I hate that I won't be able to make that choice myself, but I don't know what I'd choose even if it was offered.

"How are you feeling?" Mom asks.

"I'm alright." I smile at her as he squeezes her hand.

Mom bites her lips and tears well in her eyes. "Eira, your father and I have been talking with the doctors."

I wince. This usually ends up with yet another painful procedure done in the faint hope that it will help me. "I don't want to go through any more surgeries. I'm fine being here. I'm happy."

Mom looks away.

Dad takes my other hand, squeezing it lightly. "Unfortunately, that's not what we've been talking about. It seems as though the surgeries have done less than what we hoped. Your body is getting weaker."

A shiver runs down my spine. Yes, I have been feeling more tired lately, but I thought it was just because I'm not sleeping well.

"All the precautions we've been taking to ensure that you're comfortable here aren't enough. The air mixture can't be sustained, and if we get any sort of solar flare..." Dad shakes his head. A deep sadness comes to his eyes. "If you stay here, we'll all just be waiting for you to die."

"If I stay," I repeat, catching onto the single word that gives me hope.

Dad turns to the nearby coffee table and spreads a piece of paper over it. He hits a few buttons on the underside of the coffee table, and light glows beneath the paper, revealing it to be a map. The way the light interplays with it gives the illusion of a tiny mountain range suddenly springing to life beneath us.

"We're over the Cascade Mountains in western North America," he says, pointing. "There's a village at the top of this mountain. It was made by Aerians as the cloud descended from the peaks. They started intensive breeding programs for various types of animals that were cloned from genetic material saved from them when the cloud was first released."

"It might be possible for you to live there," Mom says. "It's several kilometers beneath us. It has a thicker atmosphere and more protection from the sun."

My heart thumps. "I will need permission from the Elder Council. But it's possible that I can breathe there? Without...?"

I glance at the oxygen tank that is my constant companion.

Mom nods. "The decision hasn't been made yet but—"

I cut her off by lifting my hand. My heart thuds all the stronger, but I don't need to hear anymore. Leaving Fata Morgana is unthinkable. Or at least, it was once. But there are always reports from the Elders about the scans taken of the surface below. Many places are regrowing plant life.

The poisonous cloud that drove our great-grandparents up above the fluffy white clouds has been scrubbed clean of the air. Yes, there remains pollution, which has turned most bodies of water to acid, but with the city's intensive seed-spreading efforts, most of the land is green once more.

I can't imagine what it looks like now. I've seen so many images filmed from the before. But if I can breathe? It's a chance I have to take! I might be happy here, but it's a choice I have to make every day.

I want to be happy without trying.

TWO DAYS LATER, I'm standing at the descent. My oxygen tank is strapped to my back, the mask bound firmly over my face. I'm wearing a full radiation suit to protect my delicate constitution from the sun. My mind whirls as I gaze at the glider that will take me to the surface.

Ever since the Elders gave their permission for me to go to the village and attempt to live my life there, I've been working hard. I've spent so many hours simulating flight that I'd be able to fly the glider with my eyes closed. I know what to do in case of turbulence or any other sort of hardship.

But I'm still hesitant. As much as I want to have this chance, there are still risks. For starters, though in the old days, there were planes that could take a person from the surface up into the sky. They don't exist anymore.

This is a one-way trip. If I go down to the surface, I won't ever come back. More than that, the glider that I take won't easily be replaced. The Elders have plans to build a new one, to ensure that all citizens can escape if there ever comes the need to flee Fata Morgana... but the fact is, I'm taking a precious resource.

"And you are worth it," Elder Kaleb had told me when I voiced those concerns. "This is a chance for you to live, Eira. Your life is precious."

I still hesitated until I remembered—my fate informs the fate of any children who are born after me who cannot adapt.

Now, I'm standing here with my parents and sisters around me. Tears stream down their faces, but I fight to keep my eyes dry. I don't want them to feel any worse than they already do.

I hug Mom first. "Thank you. I love you so much, and you've given me so much."

Mom hugs me back tighter, trembling. "I should be coming with you."

"No." I step back and smile at her. "No, you have three other daughters And just think about all your grandchildren, too. I'll be just fine on my own. They won't. They need you."

The guilt is all too plain on Mom's face, so I hug her again. There isn't much else I can do. It's not like I can just reassure her and that will make everything better. It's going to be terribly hard for her and the rest of the family.

Dad hugs me tightly. I see the guilt in his eyes, too, but he hides it a bit better. "I love you, Eira."

"Love you, too."

I exchange hugs and soft goodbyes with all my sisters, then get into the glider. There's just enough room for me in the pilot's seat with my bag of clothes and precious things I'm taking with me. The oxygen tank is the heaviest thing here, other than me. I arrange it in the back seat with my pack. If I didn't need it, I could have brought a lot more with me...

But no matter. I'll get everything I need from the village once I land.

"I love you," I call one last time, but my voice is caught by my mask as the cockpit closes.

I brace myself as the nose of the glider dips. Then it slides free, piercing through the clouds. I grasp the yoke tightly, panting in my commingled excitement and fear. The world outside the cockpit turns into a soft gray-white. I'm hidden from the world, and it feels as though I'm standing still, even though I can read the dials showing me how quickly I'm descending.

A sudden side wind jolts to me to the left, and I quickly correct. My body is growing heavier. With a laugh and a whoop, I realize it's because gravity is taking a firmer hold on me.

The glider slides through the clouds, and the land below is revealed to me. Shades of green I've only seen on film pop into view. The ground looks so soft with its fuzzy greenness. Even softer than the rolling tops of the clouds that I've been attuned to my whole life. I forget to breathe until the alarm watch on my wrist beeps.

I see the landing strip and angle the glider toward it. The landing is rough and jostles me, but finally, I come to a stop.

The cockpit moves back out of the way. A freezing wind blows in at me. I shudder as I wrap my arms around myself.

I climb out of the glider and grab my things. Taking a deep breath, I remove my oxygen mask... and the chill air invades my lungs, throwing me into a coughing fit. I have to put the mask back on and breathe deeply for several minutes before I'm able to stand again.

My head spins as I look around.

"Hello?" I call.

A person exits a small building nearby. Their eyes sweep me up and down, their lips lifting in a sneer as they stride over.

I shy back, blinking in surprise. What have I done to elicit such a response?

"So you're the newbie from Fata Morgana?" the person says. They snort. "I'm Mr. Robert, head of the village."

"Miss Eira," I reply.

Robert looks me up and down again. He's a tall man with brawny shoulders, even bigger than Dad.

"We don't have the resources to let you kick around doing nothing," he tells me, turning on his heel. "You'll be put in the deer barn. You're to keep them fed, watered, and warm. Come on. Let's get you started."

THREE WEEKS LATER, I'm fed up.

I expected to work. I've been doing the best I can, but even down here on the surface, I can't do much without my oxygen tank. The air is still too thin. Not to mention my life up in the sky had left my muscles underdeveloped compared to the people here. I try my best, but I get angry looks every time I have to stop to rest.

The baby animals are adorable, and I love to work with them, but it's not enough. I feel incredibly unwelcome here. I'm not even given as much food as everyone else, and I get eye rolls in response when I ask for more.

It turns out that the state of things here isn't as good as I was led to believe. The village only receives the odd supply drop from Fata Morgana because our orbit of the planet doesn't line up with the mountains often. They scrounge up what they can from the land itself, but not much grows way up here.

"What about in the valley?" I ask one day as I puff into my oxygen tank.

Robert grunts at me. "We don't go into the valley."

"Why not?"

"Because that's where the cloud lingered the most. It's still toxic," Robert says. "Are you ready to get back to work?"

I frown at him. "No. Actually, I'm not. It's clear you don't want me here, so I'm going to leave."

Robert's scowl turns to surprise. "What?"

I stand, grabbing my oxygen tank. "I'll collect the things I brought with me, and I'm going into the valley. I came here because I thought it would be easier, but I still can't breathe. I'm going lower."

"You can't. You'll die."

I stick my chin out at him. "Then I'll die. But if I don't, then you'll know that you can go to the valley, too, and stop being so afraid."

He blusters in response but doesn't stop me again. I get my things together and accept the food I'm offered to carry with me. Then I start to walk. I take the paths that we use when releasing animals, and once I'm at the release spot, I take a deep breath and continue on.

The low, spike-leafed trees of pine and spruce slowly thin out. The leaves get bigger and greener, and the ground grows more crowded with shrub brush.

When I stop for lunch and take off my oxygen tank. I arrange my food, then halt. My lungs are filling as usual. I take a deep breath and find that the air filling them feels... safe. Each breath draws in more oxygen than I knew air could give me.

I carry the tank with me the rest of the day, but I don't use it. I don't need to. When night comes, I'm at the peak of one of the lower mountains. The air is clear, and I stare over the darkening world, uncertain of where to go next.

Until I see it. A sea of stars nestled at the foot of the mountains.

A grin spreads over my face as I set up camp. Tonight, I will sleep here. Tomorrow, I'll descend to the lights. And there, I'll find my future.

3

AIDEN'S JOURNEY

AS USUAL, the bigger kids in my class are making fun of me.

"Hey, Aiden," Richmond sneers at me as he leans on my desk. "What's that you've got on your forehead? Is there a hole in your skull?"

I roll my eyes. I've learned long ago that Richmond only acts out like this when he's feeling insecure about himself. It doesn't help erase the sting of his words, but then again, he's not exactly original. He merely parrots what he's said ever since we met in preschool as three-year-olds.

"Sometimes I worry about you, Richmond," I say, pulling a falsely earnest expression. "You've known for thirteen years now that I require a lamplight to navigate. Have you hit your head recently?"

Richmond narrows his eyes, then belts out in laughter. He's a weird one. Sometimes, I wonder if he considers us friends, and these barbs are just part of that friendship.

He's the biggest kid in the class. I'm as tall as he is, but while he has enough muscle that he tricked the employment board into thinking that he was eighteen and eligible to work in the mines last year, I'm the opposite. I'm lean, almost skinny. I certainly haven't been able to develop the muscles that most people here in Bunk 37 have.

I've met Subterrans from other underground settlements, and all of them seem to have the same bulk. It was developed as part of the adaptations over the last one-hundred-five years, to better resist the thermal radiation that comes with being so deep underground.

"So what's this?" another of my classmates, Laura, asks, prodding at the thick coat I'm wearing. "Did you catch another cold?"

I frown at her. She's always mean to everyone. More often than not, she'll rag on Richmond, too. I guess today they've ganged up on me.

I don't like being in these situations. Despite the city's motto of no citizen left behind, it feels more often than not that I'm not wanted. Or maybe it's that they don't understand me. After all, the adaptations have worked perfectly on everyone in Bunk 37... everyone but me.

I'm not just unusual, I'm a drain on the community. Right now, while I'm still in school, it's not so bad, but what happens when I turn eighteen? That's only two more years, and then I'll be up for jobs. What sort of job can I take while being forced to wear all of this protective gear, though? My parents are working with the Elders, but most jobs require some level of experience in the mines, something I'll never have.

So then what? Perhaps being a teacher. My grades are average, though, and as hard as I try, I can't pull them up to the required levels.

My best friend, Pat, suddenly appears at my elbow.

"It's not Aiden's fault that the adaptations have failed him, loser," she spits at Laura, glowering. "Why don't you go back for a procedure to make your brain bigger, huh? Maybe then you'll understand that—"

"Pat." I put a hand on her shoulder.

She had a tendency to speak first and think later. I love Pat, and I'm always grateful for her support, but I have to admit that sometimes she causes more trouble than she fixes. I smile my gratitude toward her as the dim light of my headlamp glows on her face.

"We should take our seats," I say, glancing at Laura and Richmond as well. "The teacher will be here soon, anyway."

"You're only saying that because you know you can't do anything to stop us," Laura laughs, cracking her knuckles.

I try to hold in a sigh. She's in rare form today. "Laura, we all know that you despise me. Perhaps it's time you work on yourself instead of continually lashing out at others."

Pat chuckles. "Yeah. You're sore because Aiden gets better grades than you do. You will not get anywhere unless you use your brain as much as you flex your muscles."

"Pat," I say, sharper this time. I grab her arm and try to tug her away.

"I'm standing up for you," she hisses at me.

I shake my head. "You're making things harder for me."

"Better to be dumb and have the strength to actually help society than be a drain on resources like him," Laura shouts after us.

Pat rips herself from my grasp, making me stumble as she turns. She marches back to Laura, her fists balled at her sides. "Say that again. Huh? Just say it again! There are lots of jobs that don't require muscle!"

"But the ones that help society all do," Laura replies.

I slide into my chair, shaking my head. Most of what I'm best at—such as running figures in my head—is handled by technology, especially the robots that make our lives so much easier. Even working in the mines is done mostly with technology. Truthfully, strength isn't needed... only the bulk to resist thermal radiation.

Everyone has a purpose. Our value isn't tied to the labor we produce. Those are things I've heard from the Elders again and again.

Reality would say differently, though. It's not just the other students that end up with these attitudes against me.

The teacher comes in, and Laura, Richmond, and Pat quickly

scurry to their seats. Pat sinks heavily next to me and scowls at her hands.

"You need to stand up for yourself more," she whispers to me out of the corner of her mouth.

"You need to understand that standing up for myself doesn't automatically mean hostile confrontations," I reply.

I reach over and squeeze her hand, knowing she's feeling terrible. Her mouth pinches into a line, but she squeezes back. Pat is more than my best friend. She's like a sister to me. Both of us are only children, and we've lived in adjoining bunker rooms ever since we were born.

"I know you wish you could do more," I whisper as Mr. White calls for us to settle down. "I love you for that."

Pat smiles, then sighs.

Mr. White, the substitute who's been teaching us the past week, doesn't take his normal spot sitting on the edge of his desk. "Today, we're having a special field trip to the thermal reactors. We'll be taking a tour around the facility so we can develop a better appreciation for where all our power comes from."

My shoulders hunch inward, my gut twisting at once. I'm not allowed to go to the thermal reactor. Even with my protective gear, I have to stay within the upper twelve layers of the city. Any lower and I'd end up as toast.

I raise my hand.

Mr. White frowns. "Aiden. What is it?"

"I was wondering if I would join a different class for their lessons today, then," I say, lowering my hand again. "Or if there is any extra work I need to accomplish while the rest of you are gone?"

"What do you mean, the rest of us? Every student is supposed to have a tour of the thermal reactors."

I frown, but perhaps he isn't aware. "I have a medical exception. I can't—"

"You have your protective gear. Get ready to go, Aiden."

I sit still, counting to ten in my head. Mr. White isn't the first person to fail to realize the extent of my limitations. He won't be the last. Other than my gear, I look just like everyone else. Skinny, yes, but even that isn't as noticeable when I'm wearing all my bulky gear.

No, it's difficult to see that I can't do the same things that others my age can do. In terms of vulnerability, I'm more like a child half my age. I understand Mr. White thinking that I'm just making things up, though. After all, everyone else is grumbling about going to the thermal reactors. It's hot, uncomfortable, and noisy.

Nobody likes going there. Even fewer people like to work with the reactors. They make the city run, though, and so everyone needs to understand the difficulties and sacrifices that those who work with the reactor make.

Mr. White frowns at me. "Aiden, collect your things."

"I'm sorry, Mr. White, but I can't go. I have a medical exemption. I can't leave the upper twelve layers."

Everyone in the class is watching us now. Even Laura knows about how weak my constitution is. I wonder if she's gleeful about this tension between me and our teacher.

"You're not going to get anywhere in life if you don't challenge yourself," he tells me.

Irritation spikes through me. I want to tell him I won't get anywhere dead, either. Instead, I get to my feet. "It appears as though you don't believe me. May I suggest we go to the nurses' station? They can show you the official recommendations from my doctor."

Laura raises her hand now, too. "Mr. White, I have a medical exception as well," she says in a sing-song voice. "I'm not allowed to leave the upper four levels."

We're on the fifth level now. I grind my teeth as I shoot her a glare. Her expression is alight with malicious delight. Well, at least I know the answer to my question now. She's reveling in this whole situation.

"Aiden. I don't want to ask you again—where do you think you are going?" Mr. White demands as I head for the door.

"To the principal's office," I reply. "She's going to need to know what is happening here and why you refuse to believe my medical exemption."

I stride out, letting the door swing shut behind me.

I walk as quickly as I can, hoping to get to Mrs. O'Connor's office before Mr. White catches up. He's soon walking beside me, though. The heat of his glare lays heavy on me, prickling the skin covered up by layers of protective cloth.

When we get to the office, he makes me sit on the soft bench outside Mrs. O'Connor's office while he stalks in. I put on the headphones that I carry with me all the time to block out the low, throbbing hum of the city when it becomes too much.

Most people don't hear the noise from the machines, or they've gotten used to them. It doesn't really matter. This is the third time Mr. White has marched me to the principal's office. The first time was on account of these headphones. The second was because Laura blamed me for disrupting the class. And now this.

My headlamp illuminates the space around me. I'm the only one in all the schools that requires a lamp like this. The other students have gotten their adaptations to pick up on harmless forms of radiation that everyone and everything emits, allowing them to navigate in utter darkness. It's just one more way that I don't belong here. My light is a distraction for most of the kids in my class.

The door to the office opens again, and Mr. White stomps away without looking at me. I take off my headphones as Mrs. O'Connor steps out of her office. Her eyes are sad as she invites me into her office.

I have to repress a sigh as I step in and slump into the usual chair.

"I know, I know," I say. "You're sorry this happened, and you'll be having a talk with Mr. White to make sure it doesn't happen again. But it will happen again, and we both know it. Mr. White is not equipped to handle a student with needs such as mine. He shouldn't have been made a teacher at all, in my opinion."

The last bit just sort of slips out. I wince.

"Sorry," I mutter.

"I can't blame you. This has been a trying time for sure." Mrs. O'Connor sighs. "I've explained the situation to Mr. White. I've advised him to read through your file more carefully. You did the right thing by coming here, though."

I nod. "Thanks."

"You can go home," Mrs. O'Connor tells me. "I'll reach out to your parents with some work you can do for extra credit."

"Thanks," I say again.

Mrs. O'Connor smiles at me. "It's going to be okay, Aiden."

I smile back. But really, is it going to be? Because when I was a kid, people took my frailties seriously. Is it only going to get worse as I get older?

ELDER GRETA IS WAITING for me when I get home. At least, that's what I think at first. I gulp when I see her, certain that I'm in trouble. But as I hang up my overcoat—the family bunkers are on the top level of Bunk 37, so I don't need to have all my heavy layers—Mum speaks.

"What are you doing home so early?"

"The class took a trip to the thermal reactors." I pad into the small living space and frown. Dad is here, too. "What's going on?"

"Sit down," Elder Greta says gently.

I take a seat between my parents. Both of them have their brave faces on. My heart sinks. Does this mean I'm going to go through another adaptation?

"We have recently discovered that the radiation levels in the city are rising drastically," Elder Greta says. "There's been slippage along the tectonic plates, which seems to have set off a domino effect. We're not sure exactly what happened. But the effects are obvious. We are going to have to put shields in place to protect the city from the radiation."

There's only one reason Elder Greta would come here personally to deliver this news. "They won't be enough to protect me."

"No. We've run the calculations. I'm sorry, Aiden."

Dad puts his arm around me while Mum takes both my hands.

"The only chance—" Elder Greta starts.

"What about the toddlers? The babies?" I interrupt anxiously. I know I haven't gotten the adaptations to survive it, but what about the ones who are also vulnerable to radiation?

Elder Greta shakes her head. "They will be fine. You're the only one who has proven intolerant to even small amounts. The shields will be enough that these upper levels will be safe for the little children."

I sigh in relief.

"Aiden, we have more to tell you," Mum says. "We have talked with Elder Greta, and we have all agreed. You may have a chance if you go to the surface."

My eyes widen. "The surface? But it's full of acid and poison!"

"Not anymore," Elder Greta says quickly. "We have established communication with a settlement on the surface, habited by people calling themselves Helians. We didn't believe it at first, but it exists. They say the air is clean, and the soil is replenishing itself. We have made a map to lead you to this city."

I open my mouth and close it again, not knowing what to say.

"It will be wonderful, my darling," Mum says.

Dad nods. "The radiation levels will only last a year. Then you can come home."

A year. That doesn't sound too bad. I nod, fighting to keep my own brave face on. "Then I'll go. I must admit, I've always been curious about the sun."

Elder Greta stands stiffly. "I will make arrangements. Perhaps your parents can tell you more about the Helians."

She takes her leave. First, Mum and Dad only sit awkwardly. We're all dealing with a lot of emotion, so I finally clear my throat and turn off my headlamp. They'll feel better if I can't see their faces.

"I'm quite tired," I lie. "Maybe you can tell me about the Helians while I rest?"

"That sounds wonderful," Mum says.

We arrange ourselves so I'm lying stretched out on the couch. Mum stays with me, but my ears catch the slight movement of Dad leaving. He has a hard time with difficult things, so I don't say anything. After all, I know how he feels. It's next to impossible to act like nothing is happening when everything is changing.

"We know that a hundred and five years ago, a cataclysmic cloud suffocated the surface of the planet," Mum says. "Twenty-five years after that, the Helians emerged from their fallout shelter. They were driven out because they no longer had any food, and by chance, learned that the surface was habitable once more."

"By chance," I repeat.

"They were caught beneath a hostile sun, but eventually could harness the power of the sun and live in the open air. Now they live in a city they call New Vancouver, a place full of light, a place where everyone finds their niche."

Everyone? I settle my hands over my chest, my mind turning over Mum's words. I hope it's true.

EVEN THOUGH IT will be a year before I see them again, I try not to dwell too much on my goodbyes. Mum, Dad, and Pat are the only ones that I really say goodbye to. My entire class turns up to see me off. Laura and Richmond both look shell-shocked and guilty.

"I'll see you all in a year," I say with a cheerful wave. I hoist my pack up. I have my palmheld full of the schoolwork I'm meant to accomplish over the next year inside of it. "I'll bring you back some rocks from the surface."

Pat laughs and hugs me. Mum and Dad both tell me they love me.

Then I leave.

The walk takes me through the abandoned layers. These are spaces that lead slowly upward, full of broken things and empty spaces. They've all been abandoned for one reason or another; most of them because they were too close to the surface and earthquakes risked collapse.

I make it to the third layer above us by the time my watch says it's nighttime—not that there is a night down here. It's one of those turns of phrase that's a hold-on from the old days.

As I'm searching the maps I was given to find the way to the next level, a shriek pierces through the darkness. My head whips up, and I shove the map back into my pack. My hair stands on its end as I look around in the darkness. My headlamp, though turned up as high as it can go, barely penetrates the ink black around us.

I hold my breath and listen. It's so terribly quiet up here.

Then another shriek. It's coming from behind me, and I turn. Something skitters just beyond my light. I back away, images of childhood monsters in my mind. They seem all too real while I'm here in this abandoned place.

"Turn off the light," a voice shouts in the darkness. "They're drawn to light!"

"Who's there?" I yell.

"Turn it off!"

A high, keening wail pierces through the black. A scream answers it, and three pink, squirming creatures tumble from the darkness. Each one is as long as I am tall, standing on four legs reaching to my waist. Whiskers and bleary eyes twitch as they scream a horrible noise.

I turn and run. The light! The stranger said I have to turn it off. I can't hear anything over that wail, but I reach up and turn off my light. I run blindly until I knock into something tall and hard. It sends me sprawling backward. My head collides with the stone floor, and I lay there, groaning.

It's only after I'm bathed in a red light that I realize the ringing in my ears is from the blow. That wailing noise is gone.

A person bends near me. I can vaguely see them in the red light.

"Name's Shuang," the person whispers. "Er, Miss Shuang."

"Mr. Aiden," I reply, blinking rapidly.

"Nice to meet you." The girl sticks her hand in my face and pulls me to my feet.

Images of those pink things flash through my mind. "The light—"

"They can't see red wavelengths," Shuang replies.

I nod, relieved. "What are they?"

"Roose moles," Shuang says. "I thought everyone knew that. Where are you from?"

"Bunk 37."

"No kidding! I thought Bunk 37 got drowned in lava or something." Shuang whistles. When I wince, she laughs. "The Roose Moles don't like noise. They'll kill people, but not for food. I think they're one of those mutant species that was genetically created to be a food source."

I nod shakily.

We continue walking. It's quite a while before Shuang admits she doesn't know where she's going, so I pull out my maps again. Together, we figure out how to get to the next level. I learn Shuang is from Bunker 49 and that she was part of a crew that was heading to the surface, but she was separated from the rest of them. By the way, she devours the food I offer, I imagine she's been lost for some time.

"Why are you heading to the surface?" I ask her on the third day of our journey.

She shrugs and doesn't answer.

We're out of food by the time we reach the final elevator shaft. Along the way, we have scavenged enough supplies to make ourselves a long rope. Shuang vaults and somersaults up through the elevator as far as it goes, then secures it, and I follow up after.

We take hours of this, and each time, as I cling to some tiny spot on the rusted wall, I can only pray that I won't lose my grip and Shuang won't fall.

We reach the top and have to hoist a heavy metal door out of the way. Light floods in, blinding us both. I stumble free of the hatch and pull Shuang with me. My eyes sting and run, but they adjust faster than Shuang's. She has to cover her face as she sinks to the ground, moaning.

As my eyes adjust, I gape at what I see. Green all around me, blue above me. There are plants unlike any I've seen. So many of them are taller than I am! They jut to the sky, with long branches that sweep out from every side. They're utterly unlike the crops that are grown on the tenth layer of Bunk 37.

"Wow," I breathe.

There are noises behind us, and I turn. A handful of people come out of the plants. I lift a hand to greet them, but their expressions stop me. Glares are aimed at me from every angle... as are slim devices in their hands that look eerily similar to the mining guns the robots use.

"And just what are you doing here?" one of them demands, stalking forward.

4

NEW VANCOUVER

RYN WOKE WITH THE SUN. It was warm along their back and arms and the slowly brightening day brought an increased wakefulness to them. Unfortunately, the sunlight was the only place they were warm. They had grown cold under the stars, and now the ground beneath them sapped their heat.

With a groan, Ryn sat up, stretching their arms over their head. Their shoulders sagged as they rubbed the back of their next and sighed.

It had been almost three days since they left the Dome and they ached for someone to talk to. Their nose wrinkled as they stiffly got to their feet. They had seen fireworks in the sky last night—it had taken them a long time to figure out what those lights were until they remembered the old films that they used to watch with Aalton.

"Well, Aalton, I made an arrow to point me in the right direction," they said out loud, so as not to be overwhelmed with the silence. "And tonight I'm going to be smarter."

They found the arrow they had made the previous night and hoisted their pack onto their back. The few supplies they'd been able to save before leaving the Dome were fast running out but they had enough food to keep them going for another day if they were careful.

The real problem was being so cold!

"I know it takes cold to freeze the ice, but I never lived in it this long," they told a small furry creature that scampered across their trail as they walked, making sure they stayed toward the fireworks. "And last night I didn't think things through. I kept going way past dark so I could follow the lights and didn't build myself a proper sleeping nest."

The little furry thing was long gone, so Ryn lifted their face to the thin branches weaving into something of a canopy overhead. now and then, a bird flitted into their view and chirped or sang. Ryn tried to mimic their sounds back to them but it never worked.

Back in the Dome, the temperature was always an even temperature. Here on the surface, it changed dramatically depending on the sun. After only a few hours of walking, the chill from the night disappeared entirely and Ryn had to stuff their jacket into their backpack to avoid excessive sweating.

"Everything really is far too quiet," they said as they picked through the trees.

They knew these were trees because of what they'd been taught in school but they weren't at all like the thick kelp forests that they would swim through beneath the water. It was exotic and wonderful. The scent was sharp in their nose and they were certain if they had enough time, they could figure out how to build a fire.

Would fire be as hot as ice was cold?

Ryn was excited to learn everything they could about this world.

They found a thorny bush with bright red berries on it, the sort that they would often get as a treat. Raspberries those were called, cultivated from the bushes that the first Aquatics brought down beneath the ocean's surface with them.

After eating their fill of the sweet little berries, Ryn continued on. They rose over a crest and found themselves abruptly at the edge of the tree line. A dark swatch of brown dirt followed along the trees, as though someone had come along and plucked them out, the way some Elders would pluck their eyebrows to get a thin, streamlined shape.

"This has to be a road," Ryn muttered. "Which means it will take me to where the fireworks were used."

They walked when a creaking noise caught their attention. They turned to find the strangest creature trotting toward them. At first thought, Ryn was certain this was a centaur. It had the torso and head of a human but walked on four legs. Its lower half was encased in armor, flashing in the sun—

Only, not really. Ryn groaned and smacked their head as the person drew nearer. It wasn't a centaur at all but rather a person riding a mechanical, four-legged beast.

"Hello, there," the person called cheerily as they brought their beast to a stop. "I'm Mrs. Bunting but people call me Mama Bunting. And who are you?"

"Mx. Ryn," Ryn replied.

This was a good meeting. Ryn knew that in the past, people didn't always introduce themselves with their prefixes. They didn't understand how you were supposed to address someone before you knew what their pronouns were.

"What is this thing?" Ryn asked, pointing at the beast. "I've never seen anything like it."

"Oh, it's just my walking legs," Mama Bunting replied as she got down from it.

"That's very interesting," Ryn said politely.

"Are you heading to New Vancouver?" Mama Bunting asked.

"I don't know," Ryn replied, shrugging. "I've only recently come up to the surface. But I saw fireworks last night so I'm heading in that direction. Are you new to the surface, too? How long has the pollution been gone?"

Mama Bunting laughed. "Why don't you hop onto the legs here for a bit? I need to stretch out and you look tired."

Ryn found that climbing onto the legs was easy enough. The shiny bits flashed in the sun as the odd little party moved down the road. The legs moved slowly, far more slowly than Ryn could walk. It seemed like they were keeping in time with Mama Bunting.

Ryn took a moment to observe the woman.

She was only about the same height as Ryn but was much more muscular. She looked like she could lift Ryn over her head without grunting. Her hair was cropped short. It was the strangest shade of red Ryn had ever seen. They'd known plenty of Aquatics with red hair but never this shade. It was light, almost pink. Mama Bunting had put it into two braids that she tied together at the nape.

Her clothes were strange, too. Unlike Ryn's shirt, jacket, and pants, Mama Bunting wore one long shirt that was belted at her waist. Her shoes looked familiar, though. Her skin was a pale greenish color. Was that an adaptation to living up here?

"Are you new to the surface?" Ryn asked after some time.

Mama Bunting slapped her forehead. "Oh, dear me! I'm sorry, Ryn. I completely forgot you asked me anything. No. I was born on the surface."

Ryn gaped.

"The pollution was cleared from the atmosphere eighty years ago," Mama Bunting continued. "We're still working to pull it out of the land and water, but we have established a clean space all up and down this mountain range to the sea. The Elders are building new cleaners every year to expand our range."

Ryn clapped, delighted. "Oh, that's amazing! I'll have to tell—"

They cut off. They couldn't tell anyone. How could they? The Dome was gone, and they weren't even sure where the new Aquatics city actually was. They had tried not to pay too much attention to it, seeing as it was never built with them in mind.

"And what about you, Ryn? Where are you from?"

Ryn took a deep breath and explained everything that brought them here, although they carefully edited out the painting. It was so strange; they didn't want to have to answer the questions that they were asking. Maybe up here on the surface, they'd find the answers to that conundrum.

"I see," Mama Bunting said once Ryn was done. "That must have been a terrifying ordeal. We'll be in the city tonight, though. You'll have a warm, safe place to stay. Honestly, it's a good thing I found you. We've been having a bit of a problem with wolf rats coming after the local deer."

"Wolf rats?" Ryn repeated.

They had seen movies and read books about wolves and rats, but didn't know what the two of them together were.

"They're enormous creatures that come to your waist," Mama Bunting replied. "They were once rats, or at least that's what their DNA tells us. They have greedy little hands and beady little eyes, with slim pointed faces and twitching noses with whiskers. Their claws are sharp and they have wolf teeth in their mouths."

Ryn shuddered. That sounded horrifying!

"We're not sure where they came from, exactly, to have developed so rapidly over only a hundred years. We figure they must have been an adaptation that escaped from a fallout shelter and, with no competition, started breeding like... well, like rats." Mama Bunting shook her head. "They rarely go after humans, but you can never be too careful."

The day being so warm, Ryn soon found they couldn't keep their eyes open. Their chin nodded to their chest. The gentle movement from the mechanical legs lulled them to sleep.

When they woke again, they were in New Vancouver.

Ryn's jaw dropped open. They stared all around them, until able to stop as their head swiveled like an owl's, trying to take everything in. They had thought that the forest was green, but this place was even greener! Every building was covered in crawling vines, many of which bore fruit or vegetables. Every roof was flat, on which even more plants were grown.

"You'll notice that all the windows are slightly tinted," Mama Bunting pointed out as Ryn got off the walking legs again. "It's a new initiative by the Elders. We've been working on improving solar panel technology and now we can use them as windows. Before we had to rely on the ground panels and they'd heat terribly but now we have more access."

"That's amazing," Ryn said, clasping their hand. "The Dome was too deep to get much sunlight. We generated our electricity from the currents of the ocean."

"The city is set out in an orderly grid. You'll need to get to the city center to apply for citizenship; then you'll get your allotment of resources so you can establish yourself here," Mama Bunting said. "This here is our main road. If you follow it, you'll get to the city center. You'll want the big blue building."

"Thanks."

Ryn climbed off the walking legs. Their sleep had left them feeling more invigorated, and with the sun so bright overhead, they were definitely warm enough now.

"One more thing," Mama Bunting said. She pulled a small palmheld from her pocket. "Do you have a palmheld?"

"Er, I think so." Ryn swung their pack off and dug through it. With a cry of triumph, they held up the palmheld that they'd grabbed in their rush to leave the Dome.

Mama Bunting touched her palmheld to Ryn's. "There you go. I've sent you my address. If you need any help, come on around. I always have extra to spare and you'll need a job for your residency here. I've always got work to do."

Ryn smiled their thanks at Mama Bunting. Then, taking their leave, they strode down the road. The city was bustling with activity. Much of it was familiar to Ryn. Parents with children, people taking care of their houses, and other such things. It was nice to know that this place, even if it was unfamiliar, wasn't entirely alien.

The buildings all looked different, though. In the Dome, they were usually designed in a honeycomb pattern. These buildings were all more like the trees, round and rising high. Many of them had pergola tops stretching from one roof to the next, under which vined crops were grown. Very few parts of the Dome were dedicated to food, as they could simply harvest everything they needed from the sea. Here, it appeared every vertical space was used for the sake of food.

Mama Bunting wasn't the only one with walking legs. They chugged along easily, their shiny surfaces flashing. Ryn soon realizes that the flashing was because their legs were covered in small solar panels. There were many, many bicycles, too. In some places, the road was divided into four sections. Bikes going toward the city center had one path, bikes leaving had another, and pedestrians like-wise had a path inward and one outward. These sidewalks actually moved but only lasted for a few blocks.

Ryn was so distracted by how marvelous everything looked they missed the city center. It was only after walking for three hours that they finally asked someone for new directions and got pointed in the direction they had just come from.

By this time, their stomach rumbled. They'd only had the berries from this morning. They still had food in their pack, but when they passed a handful of street vendors selling food, they couldn't resist. The flavorful scents made their mouth water, and they headed toward the first one.

The first vendor worked on a large, flat griddle. Several fluffy cakes were frying and Ryn made a beeline for them.

"Good afternoon," they greeted politely. "I'm Mx. Ryn."

"Mr. Julian," the vendor replied.

Ryn smiled as their eyes zeroed in on the tasty-looking cake. "May I try some of your wares? I'm new and I haven't gotten a job yet, but I'd be more than happy to do some work for you in exchange."

Julian slapped his spatula against the griddle. "I have nothing for you to do. Move along."

Ryn's smile faltered. It was common practice in the Dome that if you didn't have the money to pay for something, you could trade labor or other goods for it. But this vendor seemed to be angry that Ryn suggested it at all.

"Oh. I'm sorry," Ryn stammered. "I didn't mean to upset you."

"What upsets me is you outsiders coming in here and demanding free things!" Julian exclaimed. He waved the spatula at them again. Drops of hot oil splashed on their arm. "You heard me. Get out of here!"

Ryn hurried away, rubbing the oil off their skin. What had that been about? Confusion swam through their thoughts. They hadn't been demanding anymore, nor were they asking for it for free. Why was the vendor so hostile?

Mama Bunting had been so nice to them. How could the city be so extreme as to have someone so friendly, and then a little while later have someone so rude?

Maybe the vendor was having a bad day. Maybe he had lost someone close to him, or maybe someone had stolen something from him.

At least Ryn still had food in their pack. They hurried away from the vendors, not wanting a repeat of that experience. It was only after they were away that they pulled out some food and ate while walking. After all, they didn't want to be accused of stealing, if that was why the vendor was so upset at them.

This time, finding the city center was easy. All Ryn had to do was to make sure not to be caught up in the moving sidewalks. They got off at the tall blue building and took a long moment to appreciate it.

It wasn't the tallest building here, but in Ryn's opinion, it was the most beautiful. It was built in a block shape with a peaked roof that pointed directly to the sky. The slanted roof was covered in solar panels. The tall walls had lattice work, on which grew more vines. No fruits or vegetables were hanging off these. They had probably been harvested recently.

The doors were thrown open in a welcoming way. Ryn headed inside and looked around. There were lines of people everywhere they looked. Many of them seemed to be newcomers like them, based on their worn, dirty clothes.

Several people wearing crimson uniforms stood here and there and behind desks. One of them approached Ryn.

"Hello, there. What brings you to the registry?"

"Um, I'm new to the city. I was told to come here, but I'm not sure what I need to do," Ryn said.

The crimson-clad person pointed to the longest line of them all. "Go ahead and wait over there. Once you've gotten your welcome package, you'll get instructions."

"Thank you."

Ryn went to join the line. As they waited, feet aching from the hours of walking they had done over the last few days, their mind turned to the Aquatics she had left behind.

Nobody knew that the surface was habitable again. Everyone was so isolated. Sometimes there had been newcomers from other undersea settlements who showed up at the Dome but it was few and far between.

Ryn sighed as they took a seat. It would be wonderful if they could call Aalton right now and tell him about everything they had seen in just the last three days.

Maybe there would be a way to integrate the undersea community and the surface again. Ryn first had to learn more about New Vancouver and find their own place in it. But maybe they'd see their friends again.

EIRA SWUNG her legs as she looked around at the crowded city hall center. She had been waiting here for almost two hours now, and it felt as though the line had barely moved. The workers here looked exhausted, which made Eira feel bad for taking up their time.

Unfortunately, there really wasn't anything she could do about it other than to wait it out. She had to get her residency permit to establish a new life here. It was surprising that the village up on the Cascade Mountains hadn't told her that New Vancouver existed here, but the people she had first met—Subterrans working in a field —apparently knew about the village.

Why wouldn't they get food from New Vancouver, though? Eira shook her head. She had spent little time in the village and had barely come to the city here. So, of course, she was going to have questions that didn't yet have answers.

She hummed to herself for a moment, then stopped when a few of the others around her gave her annoyed looks. Most people waiting in line seemed to be anxious and antsy, although there were a few here and there nodding off.

The person next to her shifted in their seat. Eira turned to them. So far she'd kept to herself, but she was getting bored.

"Hello," she greeted, holding out a hand. "I'm Miss Eira."

"Mx. Ryn," was the reply.

"Hello, Ryn. I'm new here; I came down the mountain from the village that was established by Fata Morgana. Where are you from?" she asked curiously.

Ryn gave her a funny look. "Beneath the sea. In the Dome. Where's Fata Morgana?"

"Up in the stratosphere," Eira replied, pointing heavenward. "So you're an Aquatic, right?"

"Yep."

Eira nodded, absorbing Ryn's striking appearance. Their dark skin was vibrant, smooth, and supple. Dark, tousled hair fell over their forehead, and eyes the color of emeralds peered around the room with determination. They'd be taller than Eira if they were standing, probably the same height as the adults around them. Their round face indicated they were the same age as Eira, though.

"I haven't heard of Fata Morgana," Ryn said, then smirked. "Actually, I hadn't heard of any other settlements. There were rumors of survivors in other undersea settlements, but until I came to the surface, I thought the air was still deadly."

"Oh? Why did you come to the surface if you thought it was deadly?"

Ryn winced at the question and folded their arms. "This is going awfully slowly, don't you think? I wish there were another couple of windows open."

Eira followed their gaze. There were about twenty of the little windows workers sat at, but only five of them were open.

"Maybe people are feeling sick today," she suggested.

She thought about asking again what brought Ryn to the surface, but it was clear Ryn didn't want to talk about it.

"Don't you think things are going slow?" Ryn complained.

"Yes, they are. But I don't mind. I'm enjoying looking around and there are so many pamphlets to read." She held up the dozen brochures she had already gone through. "It's wonderfully cool in here compared to outside."

Ryn hummed, then shrugged. "You're right. It is a lot cooler inside. I guess there's some temperature control."

"There is," Eira agreed. She handed one pamphlet to Ryn. "It's explained in here. The buildings are constructed to cool themselves off in hot weather and heat themselves up in cool weather, meaning they stay relatively stable through the year."

"That's good to know," Ryn sighed. "The outside changes so much! It's cold, then it's hot. I don't like it."

Eira laughed as she sorted through her pamphlets. "There's information on that, too. I guess it's a problem lots of people have when they leave their settlements. Fata Morgana was always carefully regulated—at least in the group home I lived in."

"Group home? I'm an orphan, too," Ryn said, their eyes lighting up.

"Oh... well, no, I'm not an orphan. I just couldn't be adapted to the environment and so had to have a special home to live in," she explained.

Ryn winced. "I'm sorry."

"It's okay." Eira gave her new friend a small smile and turned her attention back to the activity around her.

"Would you like to read some of these?" Eira offered the pamphlets to Ryn.

Ryn shook their head. "I'm more of an audio learner."

Eira nodded her understanding. "Would you like me to read any of it to you, then?"

"That would be great, thanks." Ryn grinned.

A handful of the people at the front of the line were taken through a tall door, allowing them all to shuffle up a few seats closer to the window.

Eira picked out the pamphlet about New Vancouver's Elder council and started to read. Elder Councils had been put into place even before the cloud so that every town and city had its own council of people who had seen so much of what had happened and so knew best how to serve its citizens. At least, that was what it was in theory.

"In Fata Morgana, we had an enormous scandal from one of our Elders a few years ago. He was giving jobs to his family members at over-inflated wages instead of to the people who had been assigned higher need," Eira explained to Ryn. "He was disgraced and forced to step down. It only works as a system if the Elders have the good of the citizens in their hearts."

"That's why the Elder Council in the Dome were all elected and everything they did in their government position had to be posted for citizen's review," Ryn said, scuffing their toes against the floor.

It seemed to Eira that Ryn was the sort of person who had a hard time sitting still. But then, from what Ryn had told her, they were used to having a whole city to roam. Unlike Eira, who had to make do with a small space where she was comfortable.

"It looks like the Elders here in New Vancouver are elected, too," Eira said. That was a strange thought to her, choosing which Elders would sit on the council, rather than the ones that came to the council after a certain age.

As she read on in the pamphlet, though, it became clear why they were elected here in New Vancouver rather than being assigned.

"Oh, that's awful! Before they returned to the surface, they were having massive, constant food shortages," Eira said aloud. "There was a time when they decided they couldn't have more children because there wasn't enough food, but it didn't help much. Most of the old, being more vulnerable, died. Only after were they able to develop new technology that allowed them to turn their unusable land into production areas, to stave off starvation for the whole shelter."

Ryn shuddered.

"And it turns out that they used these terraforming machines up here in this area so that they wouldn't go through that again," Eira continued, her eyes skimming over the pamphlet's information. "So that's why they didn't end up doing adaptations like other shelters.

Their focus was on adapting their environment, rather than adapting themselves."

"That would have been nice to have for the ocean. Now that I think about it, I bet the acidity is the reason the Dome failed," Ryn said, scowling at the floor now. "Aquata was being built in part to withstand the damaging effects of the acidity of the ocean."

"It would be nice if we could all just get together and share everything we have, wouldn't it?" Eira said, folding the pamphlet away.

She doubted that the stratosphere could be adapted like this, but if the land all over could be terraformed, then the seeding programs Fata Morgana was trying so hard with would be more successful.

It was a nice thought. Maybe, once Eira knew more about New Vancouver, she'd be able to talk to the Elders about it. After all, their technology was magnificent here. Perhaps there would be a way to get back home after all.

AFTER A FEW MORE HOURS, Eira and Ryn were nearly at the front of the line. When the person ahead of them was given their welcome package, Eira sighed in relief—but it was quickly interrupted by two red-clad uniformed staff leading a couple of frazzled-looking teenagers ahead of her.

Ryn groaned aloud.

The worker glanced over at Eira and Ryn, both of whom sighed.

"We want these two registered right away," one of the uniformed staff said. "They were found in the preserve."

The window worker hummed. "Names and pronouns?"

"Mr. Aiden, he/him," the one to the left said.

He was tall and lean, and even from their distance, Eira could sense an enigmatic aura from him. Dark hair fell messily about his shoulders and when he glanced back at her, she saw his eyes were the color of angry storm clouds. He didn't seem angry, though. Despite his haggard appearance—dirty, ragged clothes clung to him—he seemed to be very calm. His skin was the palest Eira had ever seen and lacked luster.

"Miss Shuang, she/her," the one to the right said.

She was a couple inches taller than Aiden and almost twice as broad in the shoulder. Her sleeveless tunic revealed heavily muscled arms. Her black hair was cropped short around her ears in a pixie cut. Her skin had the same pale undertones as Aiden's, though she had more rose-gold overtones that made Eira find it hard not to stare. She was just so beautiful.

"We're from two Subterran settlements," Shuang said. "We didn't know that the entrance led to a preserve. We would have gone through it anyway, though, because there was nowhere else for us to come out so you need to take that into consideration when you're deciding what to do with that entrance. We had to climb up an elevator shaft and if we'd come to the top to find it unpassable, we probably would have died."

The worker sighed. "I don't make those types of decisions, Miss. I will arrange for you to talk to one of the environmental committees. Please take them upstairs to room four."

"This way."

The two Subterrans glanced at each other. Aiden was the first to follow and Shuang trailed after, scowling.

Finally, it was Eira's turn. She hurried forward to the window, worried someone else might interrupt.

The worker had a large book in front of them. The pages were made of thin, pliable screens, under which were pieces of paper. The pen that the worker wrote with not only transcribed onto the screens, no doubt for digital purposes, but also the paper beneath. Eira had never seen anything like it before.

"Name and pronouns?"

"Miss Eira, she/her. Why do you ask for pronouns when we have our honorifics?" Eira asked, resting her arms on the lip of the small window.

The worker glanced up and sighed. "Not everyone fits easily into the ternary gender system and we seek to be as precise as possible. Age?"

"Sixteen."

The worker wrote it all down and then handed a package through the window to Eira. "This is your temporary residency and the credits you will need to get yourself lodgings and food for the one hundred days. Return within that time with proof of a job and permanent residence to move to the next stage.

Eira beamed. "Thank you! I'm so thrilled to be here."

"I hope you have a pleasant stay." The worker looked past her to Ryn.

Eira got out of Ryn's way and moved to the middle of the room, where she looked through the package while she waited. There were three cards in the package, as well as a map of the city and a small palmheld with emergency numbers already programmed in. On the palmheld were a few dozen markings for temporary lodgings. One was a hostel specifically for teenagers who came without family.

Ryn joined her shortly after, and they left the building together. Eira was glad that she had a friend to help see her through this. Even if she and Ryn had just met, having one more person who was also new and alone in this place gave her a little more courage.

"I have a place where we can go for work," Ryn said as they found a spot on the grounds to sit and look through their things more carefully. "I have her address with me."

"Good, we can check that out tomorrow." Eira looked at the sky, which was rapidly darkening. "It's almost night, though. We need to find a place to sleep before it's too late. I like the look of this hostel.'

She pointed out the one that was meant for teenagers. Ryn nodded and looked it up on their palmheld. They hummed as they flicked through it.

"Ah!" They cried triumphantly. "Look at this. We can contact them and let them know we're coming. I'll just send a message."

"Excellent," Eira said. "I'll find our best route to get there. It looks like there's an underground train that runs close over to where it is."

Ryn sighed in relief. "Good. I wasn't looking forward to that walk."

THE HOSTEL WAS RUN by Mrs. Yaella and her wife, Mrs. Ayasha. Both were short women with brown skin. Yaella had hazel-gold eyes while Ayasha had the most beautiful black eyes Eira had ever seen. Both had dark brown hair, though Yaella wore hers short, while Ayasha had hers long and curly.

"We don't have private rooms," Yaella said as she showed Eira and Ryn around. "You'll have your own bunk with these curtains for privacy, and then over here you'll find your lockers where you can keep your belongings. I know it's not the most comfortable space, but it is meant to be temporary housing."

"Where will we find permanent housing?" Ryn asked as they put their pack into the locker.

Yaella sighed. "Unfortunately, you'll have to have at least thirty days of proven work before you can apply for permanent housing. Ayasha will give you more information about getting a job and all of that."

"We might have a job lined up already," Ryn said. "Or at least, I do. I met someone named Mama Bunting on my way into town and she told me to come by."

"Ah, yes, Mama Bunting." Yaella smiled broadly. "She's a good friend of ours—we would have suggested you go to her, anyway. She's a third-generation citizen and is always eager to help newcomers find their place in the city."

Eira climbed onto the top bunk where she was assigned. It was higher off the floor than she was used to. While the room itself was pretty large, with a nice sitting area and another space with a table and cooking appliances, being cooped up in this small space for privacy was already wearing on her. She was used to having a lot more space than this.

On the other hand, she was also used to lugging around her oxygen tank, and she didn't need it down here. She took a few deep breaths, reveling in the air's sweetness.

"What about permanent jobs?" Eira asked. "If Mama Bunting helps, that must mean that she tries to get new workers. Which means the old workers have to go somewhere."

"Ah, yes. Well, when you're more established, you'll be able to look for other work," Yaella said. "And of course, your employment opportunities will depend on your education."

Ryn closed their locker and leaned against it. "Are there classes we can attend, then?"

Eira straightened up, excited. She had never been in a real class-room before.

"There are certain classes that you can go to for free. Mostly prac-tical skill classes," Yaella replied. A stormy look came to her face as she shook her head. "Unfortunately, most of it is quite expensive at the time being. There aren't enough teachers to go around. Once you're citizens, you can apply for further education covered by New Vancouver but..."

She shook her head sadly.

Eira wasn't sure she liked the idea of that. "The pamphlets said that all knowledge is free to everyone."

"It is. You can educate yourself as much as you wish, but the formal training and certificates are harder to come by."

Ryn shook their head and jumped into the lower bunk. "Ah, it doesn't matter. Not right now, at least. We can deal with that when we're not exhausted. I'm going to sleep. Night, Eira."

Yaella slipped from the room.

Eira closed the curtains around her bunk. It darkened her space enough to sleep, but her mind raced despite being so tired. She was going to have to read everything she could get her hands on.

She needed to know more about how this city worked.

6

THE CURIOUS NEWCOMERS

AIDEN GLANCED around the hostel as he grabbed his tray of food from the window. Yaelle and Ayasha had welcomed him and Shuang to the hostel late last night, after a long, drawn-out discussion with various people on the environmental committees. He'd slept hard in his little cubby bunk, which reminded him so much of home that when he woke, he had actually forgotten he wasn't at home.

"Hi, I'm Miss Eira," the girl sitting next to him said. "I recognize you from yesterday—something about the preserve. So you're Subterran, right?"

"Yes," Aiden replied cautiously.

"This is Mx. Ryn," Eira introduced, jutting her thumb to the dark-skinned teen on her other side.

Aiden nodded a greeting to them both. He could tell just by looking at them that neither of them were Subterrans.

Eira was, in a word, tiny. She was easily a foot and a half shorter than he was, with a fragile-looking frame. Everything about her screamed delicate, from her jet-black hair that cascaded down her back like moonlight and the huge, inky-blue eyes that stared at him, to her loose-fitting dress. It was a pale pink, contrasting nicely with the white-blue of her skin tones, and floated around her like a cloud.

"So you're both newcomers, are you?" Shuang asked, cocking her head toward the two teens.

"Yup," Ryn said. "You two?"

"I am," Aiden said.

He'd learned through the events of yesterday that Shuang wasn't coming to New Vancouver for the first time at all.

"I have family here and have registered before," Shuang answered with a shrug. "Couldn't get a permanent job, though, so I was sent back home. I wasn't going to stay underground for the rest of my life, though, so here I am."

She waved a hand around.

"Why didn't you go to your family, then?" Eira asked. "If they were expecting you—"

"They weren't, and it was too late last night to get to their houses," Shuang interrupted.

Ryn nodded. "What are your plans for the day, then? Eira and I are going to get work so we can start on this whole residency thing. We don't have anywhere to go if we can't stay here."

Shuang's expression briefly changed. Though she had been a fairly low-key person ever since they left, for a moment Aiden was sure he saw genuine anger in her eyes. It startled him more than he cared to admit—why would she react that way to Ryn? They hadn't done anything.

"I'll be getting to my family," Shuang said. "I'll see if they have room for you, Aiden."

"Thanks," Aiden murmured. "I'll be fine here, though, if they don't have room."

Shuang downed a glass of juice and stood. "Actually, I better get going. I want to catch them before they head out into the fields. You can call me on my palmheld, right?"

Aiden nodded.

"Good luck. I'll keep in touch," Shuang said and then left, her footsteps solid and heavy.

Aiden couldn't help but feel like there was something huge he was missing here. Maybe Shuang didn't have a good relationship with her family. Maybe there was bad blood here because she hadn't been able to get a permanent residency in New Vancouver and had to leave again.

Yaella came over to collect Shuang's left-behind tray. "How is your breakfast, Aiden?"

"It's delicious," Aiden replied. "I haven't ever had potatoes cooked this way before."

"I'm glad. You'll find that most of the food here in New Vancouver is going to be different from what you were used to below ground. Most newcomers find it a little challenging to adjust to. But I suppose that's mostly because newcomers are so rare; with time there will be larger communities within New Vancouver that share their recipe books."

Ryn grunted as they polished off their plate. "We should get going if we want to find work."

"Why are newcomers rare?" Eira asked, as though she hadn't heard Ryn.

Yaella shrugged delicately. "Well, if you think about it, most settlements are rather isolated. Look at Ryn, here. They thought that the atmosphere was still poisonous. Then look at you. Most Aerians are adapted to the stratosphere. Even your skin is designed to deflect a higher abundance of UV rays."

"Is it?" Eira looked at her arms. "So this is an adaptation? No wonder I look different from everyone in my family."

Aiden chewed his food thoughtfully. What Yaella said made sense. Much of the Subterran bunkers and shelters had expanded within themselves, but few interacted with one another. Why was that? He couldn't think of any reason they couldn't have contact with other settlements. But that one time Mrs. O'Connor tried to arrange for the school to have pen pals with another bunker, it was shot down pretty quickly.

"Yes, there's that," Ayasha said as she came up behind Yaella.

"But also New Vancouver doesn't make it easy for newcomers to adapt."

Aiden's stomach clenched, threatening to expel the food he'd just eaten. There were more adaptations that he'd have to go through here? But the reason he had had to leave home was because the adaptations hadn't taken.

The many, many painful procedures he'd endured to make him more suitable for below-ground living flashed through his mind. His hand tightened over his spoon and he felt the blood draining from his face.

"Are you okay?" Ryn asked him, reaching over to support him.

Aiden shook his head. He carefully got out of his chair and laid down, letting the cool floor soothe his nausea. "I didn't realize we had to adapt. I don't want to go through any more surgeries. I'm only supposed to be here for a year, anyway."

"I don't want to go through more adaptations, either," Eira said. Her voice was high and thin, just as frightened as he felt.

"Oh, no, that's not what I mean," Ayasha said.

Aiden peered up at her.

Her expression was twisted in regret. "I'm sorry, I forgot. In New Vancouver, we don't do adaptations like what you're familiar with. There are no procedures or surgeries. I meant adapt behaviorally. New Vancouver has certain requirements for residents to get citizenships, and it requires a change in behavior and thought processes which are often difficult for newcomers to do."

Aiden's lungs loosened a little. He let his eyes shut as he breathed to regain equilibrium. Once he was certain he wasn't going to pass out, he got back into his chair. He was left feeling shaky as he sat there.

No more procedures. That was good. He didn't think he'd be able to make it if there was something like that he'd have to undergo here. None of the adaptions below ground took, and he was terrified that he'd find he had no place here, either.

It was only after he sipped some water that he realized Eira looked slightly green. She rested her head in her hands, her eyes closed. Ryn's hands were clasped in their lap as they stared ahead stonily.

"Neither of you could adapt either, could you?" he asked, understanding the same emotions he had just gone through.

Eira shook her head.

Ryn let out a heavy breath. "No. I couldn't adapt. The Dome was fine for me since it was built for the first ones who left the surface and they weren't adapted, either. So I didn't have to go through too much... but..."

They shuddered.

Yaella's eyes gazed into the distance, her hands clasped tightly in her lap. Aiden wondered what she was remembering—he thought both Yaella and Ayasha were Helians. If they didn't undergo adaptations, what would cause that expression on Yaella's face?

"Well, never mind," Ayasha said, an arm around Yaella's shoulders. "You three will be just fine. You're all bright and eager. I'm sure that you will adjust and learn quickly."

Aiden opened his mouth to ask more questions, then stopped. If he was honest, he wasn't sure that he wanted more answers. Not yet, at least. He needed to take some time to properly absorb what had already been said so he could know the right questions to ask.

He was feeling much better now, so he took his tray to the counter and headed back to the room. There wasn't anywhere in the sleeping rooms to change, so he grabbed fresh clothes and went into the bathroom to get out of his sleeping clothes.

Soon, he, Eira, and Ryn had left the hostel. They headed for Mama Bunting's place. As they walked, Aiden deliberately turned his mind from the conversation with Yaella and Ayasha, instead considering 'Mama Bunting'.

Where had the name 'Bunting' come from, anyway? To Aiden, it sounded like some sort of dumpling, but when he looked it up on his palmheld he found it was actually a type of bird, or a decorative flag, or a sleeping bag for babies. None of that told him why someone would name their child Bunting, although he supposed names like Wren or Sparrow were common enough, and those were types of birds.

"What do you think they meant?" Ryn asked suddenly.

Aiden looked up from where he was reading. They were on one of the moving sidewalks, heading toward the outskirts of the city.

"I don't think it's something for us to worry about yet," he said, knowing that Ryn was talking about the conversation with Yaella and Ayasha. "It's best if we find our footing first before we look to answer questions."

"Or maybe we should find our answers, so it's easier to find our footing," Ryn said. Their expression twisted as they lifted their face toward the bright blue sky. "Now that I think about it, why do we have to have a permanent job and residence before we become citizens? Shouldn't we become citizens and then be given permanent jobs and residence?"

Eria, her face buried in her palmheld, shook her head. "Maybe it's so that people are serious about it."

"Maybe we should just go to the Elder Council and find out ourselves," Ryn said.

Aiden gaped at them. "You don't just go to the Elder Council like that!"

"Why not?" Ryn folded their arms and tapped their toes. "They're meant to be looking out for us, aren't they? We're only teenagers."

"You mean we're already teenagers," Eira replied. She tucked her palmheld away.

Ryn turned their frown on her. "What do you mean by that? We're all sixteen—"

"I'm seventeen," Aiden interrupted.

Ryn shrugged. "Sixteen, seventeen. It doesn't matter. We're still teenagers. In the Dome, we weren't considered emancipated adults until we were at least twenty-five. Although we had chores like cleaning the air scrubbers and the like."

"But twenty-five is so old," Eira protested. "In Fata Morgana, we're expected to get jobs and start contributing as soon as we turn fifteen. Earlier, if we can. We're allowed all the same rights as adults as soon as we're contributing to taxes."

"Fifteen?" Ryn repeated, looking aghast.

Eira turned to Aiden. "What about in Subterra?"

Aiden folded his arms. "There are dozens of different cities below the earth. In mine, we were allowed to start having jobs at fourteen if we so wished, but were provided for by the city until we turned thirty."

"Huh," Ryn said. "Weird, isn't it? How different we all are. Wonder what the norms here are... other than making newcomers get a job, that is."

The three of them lapsed into their own thoughts until they came to the end of the sidewalk. They stepped off and stuck together as they moved through the crowd. Ryn, palmheld in hand, led them toward Mama Bunting's place. Soon they came to an open-air market.

The scent of spiced food made Aiden's stomach rumble. Although breakfast had been delicious, the spike of anxiety there at the end had prevented him from finishing it.

"Why don't we get some snacks?" he suggested as they passed through a vendor with fluffy cakes frying on a griddle.

"Yeah, those look delicious," Eira agreed.

As they both started toward the vendor, though, Ryn grabbed their arms. There was an uncertain, almost frightened, look on their face. It looked so out of place in the time Aiden had known them he looked around for some sort of wild animal.

"What is it?" Eira asked.

"Yesterday when I came through, I asked that man if I could do some work for him in exchange for some food, and he got very aggressive with me. He was acting like I was trying to steal from him."

"What for?" Aiden asked, surprised.

Ryn shook their head, narrowing their eyes at the vendor, who seemed to ignore the group. "I don't know, but I don't trust them."

"It must have been just a bad day," Eira said.

"That's what I thought, but I'm not so sure."

Aiden considered a moment, then nodded, his mind made up. "Let Eira and I go over first, then. If he's still grumpy, we'll get some food somewhere else."

Ryn hung back while Aiden and Eira went to the vendor. He kept ignoring them even after they were standing right in front of him.

"Excuse me," Eira said brightly. "We would like to buy three cakes. We have credits."

She held out her card, and the vendor looked up with a nasty look on his face. "Really, credits? Then I'll have to go through all the hoops of exchanging them for real money."

"We were told it automatically transferred," Aiden said, shocked.

"You can't expect to come in and take things from people who have worked their whole lives in this city," the vendor said.

What did that have to do with anything that they had just been talking about? Eira and Aiden shared a startled glance.

"I'm sorry," Eira said, her voice lowering. "We didn't mean to cause you any trouble. We just wanted to try one of those cakes. But we are looking for work, too. We're—"

"I don't have any work for you. Get out of my face!" the vendor snarled.

Aiden put an arm around Eira's slender frame and moved her back, stepping in front of her. He glared at the vendor, who glared back. The two teens left without another word—Aiden wasn't sure why the man was so hostile toward them, but he had an inkling.

This interaction paired with Ayasha's warnings earlier in the day... Was this what she meant by New Vancouver, making it difficult for newcomers?

They were quiet the rest of the way to Mama Bunting's place. It was a cute little café with an open-air patio where a bunch of customers sat sipping at their drinks or nibbling at pastries.

Mama Bunting, who looked pretty much exactly as Ryn had described her, greeted them all warmly.

"I'm busy right now, but after hours I'll start teaching you three how to take orders and prepare the coffee," she told them.

"Coffee?" Aiden repeated.

He straightened. The coffee supply back home was carefully rationed; it was only passed out on New Year's Eve. He sniffed the air and the earthy aroma made his mouth water.

"What's coffee?" Ryn asked.

"It's a bean that you grind up and make into a drink to wake you up," Eira replied. She frowned. "I wasn't ever allowed any because of my delicate constitution. Maybe it's different down here?"

Aiden smacked his lips. "It's delicious, Ryn. The best thing in the entire universe!"

Ryn gave him a funny look while Mama Bunting laughed. "Yes, Subterrans tend to have a deep love for coffee. But anyway, let's get you started with your first day of work, shall we?"

The three teens followed her around the café, where she pointed out buckets of paint and some gardening supplies. She instructed them to paint the little fence around the garden and then carefully pull out the weeds.

Ryn and Eira seemed to know what plants were weeds and what were supposed to stay but Aiden stuck with the painting. He hadn't ever worked in a garden before, despite them being on a level he could visit.

Mama Bunting scanned their work credits to show they had started, then left them to it.

Eira talked brightly, telling the other two about the books she had read. Ryn seemed to be very invested in the story. Aiden, on the other hand, took the opportunity to think. He was used enough to Laura and Richmond teasing him he could easily tune out Eira's voice.

What was his family doing right now? What about Pat? Were things feeling as odd and new for them as they were for him?

And what about Shuang? Where had she gone? Why did he feel like there was a lot she wasn't saying? Why would she come back to New Vancouver when it seemed as though she hated it?

It made little sense. But one thing did—this utopian world wasn't as perfect as it first appeared to be.

7

CAFÉ CONVERSATIONS

WORKING in a café was strange to Eira. She had never even been to a café before, let alone work at one. She found it an amazing adventure. It seemed to her like the café was a hub for people of all walks of life. She learned more about people and New Vancouver just from talking than she ever could from reading.

It was beautiful. Eira loved the work. She loved interacting with people, taking their orders, fixing problems for them, and all of that.

Aiden was very polite to everyone but didn't engage with the customers the same way she did. He admitted he found it quite draining, so the two of them quickly figured out if someone coming in wanted a cheerful conversation or quiet contemplation. They traded off these customers and soon had their favorite regulars.

Ryn, on the other hand, was very popular, but grew bored with taking orders and cleaning up after customers. Mama Bunting took them into the kitchen; there was constant work to be done in there and Ryn thrived in it. They could accurately guess how much they needed to bake, and even being interrupted by custom orders, kept the display cases filled.

"You three are doing an excellent job," Mama Bunting said one afternoon during the slowest time of day. "I'm very pleased with your progress after only three weeks."

Eira finished wiping down the counter she was cleaning and then leaned against it. "Thank you. I've been going to other cafes and vendors to see if I can find permanent work with them. It seems like most everyone is using robots and the like for taking and making orders."

"Yes, most people do," Mama Bunting said, nodding. "One reason why my place is so popular is because it has the human touch, but there are always benefits from going somewhere that you know exactly what will happen every time."

"I don't think I want to make a career out of the kitchen, anyway," Ryn sighed. They were at a table, spinning a spoon on its end. "I just don't know what to do. I've been trying to read those job opportunity pamphlets, but none of them make any sense."

Eira winced. She had been reading them aloud to Ryn, but it was true. Everything was written so confusingly, it was as though the Elders didn't want people to find full-time employment.

Mama Bunting nodded sympathetically. "I know what you mean. Most of those jobs require previous education."

Aiden, who was refilling the sugar, grunted. "Seems to me that the best way to keep busy and have a job is to start up your own business. But you have to be a citizen before that's recognized. I'm thinking the only opportunity for full-time employment for me is in the fields with the other Subterraneans."

A customer entered the shop and came to the counter. Aiden and Mama Bunting kept cleaning while Ryn took the spoon they'd been playing with into the back.

Eira stood behind the counter to take the customer's order. They were an Aerian like her, but looked far more wary. The blue tones of their skin were more pronounced than hers, too. They ordered their coffee to-go and soon the café was dead again.

"Guess we've gotten everything done around here that needs to be done right now," Aiden mused. "The garden is free of weeds, there's nothing to harvest, the windows are cleaned, the floor is swept..."

Mama Bunting laughed. "Then head on upstairs for your lunch."

Eira smiled gratefully. She put a quick sandwich together for herself and headed upstairs. Aiden was quick to follow her, and they settled down with their food. Ryn, it seemed, had found something to busy themselves with.

"You know, I noticed Subterrans stick together, and so do Aerians. Don't see many Aquatics, though," Eira mentioned as she ate.

"I noticed that too. I figured it was because they were coming in with the friends they had before they came to New Vancouver," Aiden answered.

He chewed thoughtfully, his eyes sharp. Something about them told Eira that he had more thoughts on the matter but wasn't ready to share them just yet. That was one thing that Eira found pleasant and annoying all at the same time. Aiden was a deep thinker and talked little unless he was absolutely certain about what he was saying.

"But you think it's more than just that they're friends before coming to New Vancouver?" Eira pressed.

Aiden shrugged. "Maybe."

"Tell me."

Aiden grinned at her and shook his head. "Maybe not."

Eira huffed and rolled her eyes. Fine. If he didn't want to tell her, she'd figure it out herself.

AFTER LUNCH WAS ANOTHER RUSH. A group of familiar Subterrans, whom Aiden usually served, came in and sat in the corner. Aiden was busy with another customer, so Eira grabbed her notebook and headed over to them.

"Hello! You look like you've been out in the sun. Can I suggest a refreshing cool drink?" she asked.

One of them, Mr. Fred, frowned slightly at her. "Four ice waters and potato skins, please."

"I'll put that right in," Eira said.

She took the order back to Ryn in the kitchen and then prepared the water herself. Aiden came over to help her, but she shooed him away.

"I don't have anyone else right now," she told him, then lowered her voice. "Besides, how can I get to know other Subterrans if I never have them as customers?"

Aiden shrugged and stepped into the back.

Eira carried the water to the table and handed it out. "Have you all been out in the fields?"

Fred snorted. "Of course."

"Of course?" Eira asked, frowning. "I'm sorry. I didn't mean to—"

"It's fine. I don't expect an Aerian to understand," Fred said, waving his hand.

Eira winced. She worried her lip between her teeth, then blurted, "I know I'm new here. I don't understand at all—can you help me understand? I just don't want to offend anyone in the future."

The Subterraneans glanced at each other. One of them, Miss Helga, turned to her.

"It's like this, Miss Eira," she said, her tone flat. "There are limited jobs that newcomers can get here unless they have specialized education. For Aerians it's entertainment and serving jobs. For Subterrans, it's physical labor. Building, farming, all that. People look at our muscles and decide the only thing we're good for is throwing things around. Even with education, it's difficult to get out of the fields."

Eira's eyes widened. "But that's not fair!"

Helga's lips twitched. "No. It's really not. But it is what it is. What can we do about it? At least we're not overrun by wolf rats."

"It's still not fair. I thought... I thought that once we become citizens, we get to benefit from New Vancouver," Eira said.

"We do. We have everything we need," Fred said with a shrug.

"We work less up here than we would have to below the surface and we have the benefit of the city's protection. Doesn't mean it's perfect."

LATER THAT NIGHT, after a long day's work, Eira was lost in her thoughts as the three teens headed back to the hostel.

"You're being awfully quiet," Ryn said as they approached the marketplace.

Eira looked up. "Oh, just trying out my best Aiden impression, I guess."

"Hmmm," Aiden said, fighting a grin. "That must mean you were deep in your thoughts. Care to share how it worked out?"

"Not well," Eira admitted.

Ryn slung an arm around her shoulders. "Maybe sharing out loud will help?"

Eira considered. That might be something, after all. "I'm thinking about what the Subterrans told me this afternoon. That just because they're bulky, their jobs are all physical labor. But there are so many robots for that. So is the city creating those jobs just to push Subterrans into it?"

"I thought the opposite," Aiden replied. "That they created the jobs so the Subterrans would have work to become residents."

"It's still awful, making it so that's the only work they can do. I don't understand why the Elders don't open up more teacher jobs or create a program so there can be more teachers if that's the reason education is so limited," Eria said. Her brow furrowed, and she rubbed her forehead. "It just seems like we could all be Helians, that it's our natural space. But..."

She trailed off, shrugging. The adaptations had changed Subterrans, Aerians, and Aquatics that was for sure. Nobody in the past had this blue tint to their skin like she did. Aiden and Ryn's colorings seemed more natural, but even they had changes done to them through the adaptations.

They passed by that awful cake vendor who glared at them like he did every day. They weren't even doing anything to him, and he acted like they had kicked him in the head.

Eira shook her head.

"It's not just that," Ryn muttered, glaring at the ground. "Look at how everything is set up. The city isn't built to integrate newcomers.

The three fell back into a weighty silence. Eira didn't like thinking the worst about the Elders but that's what it felt like. Her chest hurt the more she thought about it but she couldn't get herself to think about something else.

Especially when they returned to the hostel and found a new teen there. This newcomer was younger than the three of them and sat at the table, head in their arms as they sobbed. Yaella sat next to the teen, rubbing their back soothingly.

Aiden and Ryn slipped quietly into the rooms, but Eira hesitated. Maybe there was something she could do…

She approached, wringing her hands. "Is there anything I can do to help Yaella?"

"Can you make some tea, please?" Yaella asked. "Ayasha is making supper."

Eira nodded and headed into the kitchen.

Ayasha had already put a tea bag in the cup and was working at the stove as she waited for the water the boil.

"Yaella asked me to bring out the tea for the new teen," Eira explained.

Ayasha nodded. "Thanks. It's an awful situation—the family was rejected for residency except him. They just came up from an Aquatic city, hoping to live as Helians."

"Why?" Eira asked quietly.

Ayasha hummed. "Apparently, the youngest child is having trouble with adaptations. The city gave them six months for Riley to establish himself as capable of caring for his sibling before sending the parents away again."

"But he has to be younger than me. How can he care for a child?" Eira asked, aghast.

"There will be resources to help him... but only if he can establish base care." Ayasha shook her head, her eyes hard. "I don't know what's wrong with this city sometimes. We have more than enough— oh. But this isn't your burden."

Ayasha patted Eira's shoulder as the kettle whistled. She poured the tea and sent Eira off. Eira gave the sobbing teen the tea and headed to her bunk.

She closed her curtains off, not wanting to pretend to be in a good mood. But her mind was filled with doubts. Was New Vancouver as good as she had thought? Why were things here the way they were?

Was there anything she could do to make it better?

8

THE ELDER COUNCIL

RYN PULLED a scarf around their throat, grimacing at the dark cloud cover outside their window. They and their new friends hadn't experienced storms until coming to New Vancouver, as Ryn and Aiden had both been below the surface and Eira above the clouds. Yaella and Ayasha had to explain the weather to them and how to dress for it.

"Are you ready to go?" Eira asked from the front of the room.

"Tell Mama Bunting I'm not coming in today," Ryn answered as they turned around.

They felt a bit guilty about it, as the café was getting busier every day. There was something else they had to do. They had stayed behind late last night with Mama Bunting to help with closing while Eira and Aiden came back here. Ryn had explained to her exactly what she was planning and only said that they hadn't decided when to do it yet.

Last night, they had been tossing and turning all night, so they knew—today was the day.

"Are you feeling okay?" Aiden asked Ryn, frowning.

Ryn grinned in return. "I'm fine. I just have some things to do."

"What?" Eira asked.

Aiden's gaze seemed to burrow right through Ryn, but they turned away and grabbed a pair of light gloves.

"It's personal, for the time being," Ryn replied. They didn't want their friends to get caught up in this or try to talk them out of it.

Eira looked worried, Aiden suspicious, as the two of them left. Ryn let out a sigh of relief and tugged on the gloves. A light rain was falling outside, and they tucked their hair under their knitted hat. Would the Elders even see them? Here, they weren't even a citizen. It wasn't like back under the Dome, where they were a ward of the state and so close to the Elders.

"If they don't let me see them, I'll just have to camp out on their steps until they do," Ryn muttered to themself. Elder Valdimar always said they were quite the stubborn one, and that stubbornness could do great things if Ryn used it the right way.

They hoped this was the right way.

They wished they could talk to Elder Valdimar now. They wished Aalton was here. Eira and Aiden were great, but they weren't family... yet, at least.

Taking a deep breath, Ryn headed out into the light storm. The air smelled all wrong with the rain, like a burned-out air scrubber. It made their nose itch and Ryn scrubbed at it with their palm. They soon figured out to keep under the slight lips from the buildings over the sidewalk to keep dryer, but were still soaked through by the time they reached the city center.

Rather than the blue welcoming building where Ryn had gone on their first trip, they headed to a green one at the back of the city center. It was shorter than the others, though no less beautifully built. It was made of stone, cut into blocks and fitted together perfectly. The vines and ivy that grew up around it were laden with small berries that didn't yet appear to be ripe. Garden boxes full of legumes and starch vegetables surrounded the building.

Ryn was welcomed in, and when they requested to speak with the Elders, the crimson-clad worker frowned at them.

"Do you have an appointment?" the worker asked.

"No. Do I need one?" Ryn asked, pinching their brow together. "I looked up everything I could find and asked some people around. They said nothing about needing an appointment."

The worker sighed. "I suppose that's true. You don't technically need one. But the Elders are very busy today. Give me your citizen number and we'll get back to you."

"I don't have a citizen number. I'm still a resident," Ryn explained.

"You're not Helian?" the worker asked, a note of disapproval creeping into their voice.

Ryn swallowed. "No. I'm a newcomer from the Aquatics. I came from the Dome. I guess New Vancouver doesn't know about the Dome yet, but I have my registry. Mx. Ryn. I can—"

They pulled out their residence card when the worker snorted. "The Elders are much too busy to meet with a kid like you."

Ryn's jaw dropped. Why was the worker being so rude? The temperature had dropped noticeably. Ryn rubbed their arms, but knew the coldness wasn't because of the icy rain outside. It was toasty warm in here and there was no reason for it to have suddenly gotten colder.

The worker was ignoring them now. Ryn almost turned to go, but remembered the painting. They did not know how to go about figuring out that mystery, but remembering it made them think about how hard it was to leave the Dome. They had done something they hadn't thought was possible when they did that. How much more difficult could it be to speak to the Elders?

"I need to speak with them," Ryn repeated. "It's my right to have my voice heard. Residents are not supposed to be treated with less hospitality than citizens. It's in the New Vancouver charter."

"Hospitality doesn't mean you can simply barge in on the Elders when they're busy," the worker said brusquely.

"Can you at least let them know I'm here?"

"What is going on?" a stern voice behind Ryn turned.

"Elder Suzanne." The worker straightened. "Mx. Ryn here is a resident who wants to speak with the Elders. I told them—"

They cut off at a wave from Elder Suzanne's hand. "Mx. Ryn. I'm Elder Suzanne, she/her."

Ryn bowed politely to the intimidating woman. Her hair was pure silver, deep wrinkles etched into her beautiful face. Her eyes were the deepest black Ryn had ever seen and her skin was a lovely, burnished gold color. She looked like a wise heroine from days of yore.

"Elder Suzanne, I recently arrived in New Vancouver from the Dome; it's an aquatic city that recently failed. Everyone was moved to a new city, except for me, because I couldn't adapt to the environment," Ryn said. "There are some—"

"Regardless of where you come from and how things are done under the Dome, you are being rude," Elder Suzanne cut across them, folding her arms.

Ryn flinched. "I didn't realize I was being rude."

"Then you should learn more about your new culture before you demand things—"

"It's as a newcomer here that I can show a new viewpoint," Ryn interrupted. "You see, there are problems—"

Elder Suzanne gave Ryn a sharp look, making their words die on their tongue. "Mx. Ryn, the Elders are very busy today. Leave your name with Alex here and we will get back to you when we can see you."

Ryn ducked their head. They wanted to double-check to ensure that the Elders would talk to them, but with how upset Elder Suzanne seemed to be, they decided not to risk it. It was better than nothing, and if they pushed too hard, then the Elder might get even madder at them.

"Thank you," they muttered and turned back to Alex. Hopefully, this would go somewhere.

DAYS LATER, Ryn wondered If they should have been more pushy. So far, there had been no word from the Elders as to when they would call Ryn to see them. It was beginning to feel like it was never going to happen.

Eira put an arm around Ryn's waist, hugging them. "I know that waiting is hard. I'm sure that they just need to find time. I'm sure they're very busy."

"Thanks," Ryn said, slinging an arm around Eira's shoulder. They didn't point out how Eira had been sure of the same things every day so far.

It was their day off from Mama Bunting's café, so the three of them were taking the time to explore the city and learn more about it. Currently, they were going through the trades-training spaces. They had stopped in at a few schools only to be disappointed to learn that the free hours were all booked up already.

"It's annoying that we're being put to work instead of continuing our education," Aiden grumbled. "So many of the uneducated jobs can be taken by robots. Why shouldn't they be freed up so we can educate ourselves and take on more meaningful employment?"

"Let's keep going," Eira suggested. "It looks like there's a school over there. We'll find a way to do both."

Run smiled, soothed by their friend's optimism. Aiden still looked disheartened, but not as bad as he had moments ago. They quickly made their way to the school and entered.

The building was silent, and they peered through the doors of various classrooms as they looked for whoever was in charge. Teachers and students both worked hard, not noticing them. Finally, they found the principal's office. The principal first thought that they were students, but after the three explained the situation, the principal introduced himself as Mr. Howard.

"Is there any way we can enroll ourselves here?" Aiden asked.

Mr. Howard sighed heavily as he shook his head. "I'm afraid that since you aren't citizens, you aren't able to receive a free education here, at least not in our traditional classrooms."

Aiden slumped in his seat. Ryn hated seeing him like that, so they leaned forward and narrowed their eyes, studying the principal. "Once we are citizens, we can come back, then?"

The principal winced. "Unfortunately, you'll still have to pay. The free education program is only for the children of citizens. If you're a first generation, you get a certain percentage off once you're a full citizen. But our free living programs were recently reduced, so you'll still have to work to afford your housing. I'm sorry. We're struggling with our resources."

Ryn frowned. Struggling? New Vancouver seemed to have more than enough for everyone!

"Aren't there any sort of grants that we can apply for?" Eira asked. "All three of us are without family here. What are we supposed to do?"

Mr. Howard shook his head, regret on his face. "I'm sorry. I've got my hands full with running this school and trying to ensure that all our students have the learning resources they need. But all our materials are free on the palmheld network. If you want to self-educate, you can sign up for exams which are much cheaper than the full course."

Aiden got to his feet. "Thank you. We'll leave now."

Ryn thought they could still demand more answers or at least learn more about online learning, but Aiden looked so upset they didn't argue. The three of them left the school, heading back into the open air. It was another muggy day.

"I miss my home," Ryn sighed. "I miss Aalton and the Elders I knew. But they don't even know if I'm alive."

Eira turned to them as the three headed back toward the hostel with Aiden leading. "I forgot. You haven't told us how you got up here."

Ryn grinned. "Well. It's certainly strange. Let me start at the beginning. My friend Irta was sick..."

BACK AT THE HOSTEL, the three of them sat around the table while the painting from under the Dome lay flat in front of them. They had discussed various means of how someone long ago could have known about Ryn to paint them. So far, it ranged from coincidence to a magical fairy portal.

"In Fata Morgana, we don't get lightning often," Eira said, resting her elbows on the table. "But to us, it's a sign of change. A symbol used when there were city-wide protests when the council was debating the first seeding programs."

"For or against?" Aiden asked.

"Some against, mostly for." Eira touched the painting. "Maybe there is something magical about this, Ryn. Maybe you're meant to bring change to New Vancouver."

Ryn scoffed, their cheeks turning hot. They were glad that their dark skin would hide the blush from Aiden and Eira's eyes. "I'm not some leader of change. I bet Elder Valdimir was just making up stories to give me hope. He was just trying to make me feel better about leaving."

They grabbed the painting and started rolling it again. They missed the Dome. But could Eira be right?

No. No, Eira wasn't right. Ryn was just Ryn. They weren't about to change a whole city.

FINALLY, Ryn was called to speak to the Elders.

The Elder's Council chambers were a narrow, long room with a table that ran down the center. The various Elders sat along either side of the table. Binders and papers and palmhelds were all out in front of them. Some Elders smiled in welcome, while others seemed a bit annoyed.

"Thank you all for seeing me," Ryn said, bowing. "I have a few things I would like to speak to you—"

"Mx. Ryn," Elder Suzanne interrupted. "It is customary to keep your tongue until all the Elders have been introduced."

Ryn bit their tongue, fighting back a well of shame.

Another Elder sighed. "Suzanne, please. You are being rude to our guest." The Elder then smiled at Ryn. "My name is Elder Fraces, he/them."

They continued around the room, with everyone introducing themselves. Ryn made a point of memorizing each name and the face it went to. Once they were done, Ryn could speak. They brought up Aiden's concerns about having too much work to dedicate to education.

"We are struggling with our educational resources," Elder Frances said with a nod. "Which is why we have all the information made available free."

"It's still inaccessible to people like me who have difficulty reading," Ryn replied.

Elder Frances hummed. "We are hiring people to read aloud all the information we have collected over the years. Our laws are in place to ensure that there remains enough vital resources for everyone."

Ryn crossed their arms and then dropped them back to their sides, not wanting to look confrontational. "That's not what it looks like. It looks like you're hoarding resources for the people who lived here first."

"Not the necessary resources," Elder Suzanne was quick to say. "Food, water, shelter, clothing. It's available for everyone."

Elder Manny spoke up, stroking his silver mustache. "Some would argue that education is a necessity for today's world."

Suzanne shot him an angry look.

Ryn's stomach clenched. Were the Elders divided? They couldn't tell if this was personal or professional. They took a deep breath and squared their shoulders.

"There's more. The laws on residency and citizenship... they're pushing separation. The Subterrans who come here almost always end up in the fields, despite their education from their homes. But they need to pay to prove their education and the test dates are set up in such a way—"

"Mx. Ryn. Is the reason you came to see us just to rehash things that we have already made statements on?" Elder Suzanne demanded. "We have our laws and the reasons for each law available for you to pursue."

"Yeah, but you don't know how your laws are impacting people directly," Ryn said boldly.

Suzanne shook her head. "Our city is barely eighty years old. It's still fragile and we have only so much room to grow. We can't just take on anyone who wants to come here. I'm sorry that you don't seem to understand that."

Ryn was summarily dismissed. They turned with stooped shoulders, feeling defeated. How could they reason with the Elders if the Elders wouldn't even listen?

9

A GROWING DISCONTENT

AIDEN STRETCHED out in the hostel's courtyard, soaking up the last rays of sun. From his research, the radiation from the sun could be dangerous, but it posed a much smaller risk than the thermal radiation he'd been exposed to below the surface. The warmth felt good on his skin, and he imagined that his pale tones had darkened a shade or two. It was difficult to tell but the whole possibility fascinated him.

"Hey," a voice said somewhere above him.

With a lazy yawn, he opened his eyes, expecting to see Eira. To his surprise, it was actually Shuang who stood over him. He leaped to his feet, beaming.

"Hey! I didn't think you were coming to see me until tomorrow," he said.

Shuang shrugged, though she looked pleased. "I couldn't stop thinking about how you're stuck working at that café. It's not really an important job and I'm worried that you'll be denied citizenship at the end of your residency if you don't have something better."

"The packet I was given just said I needed permanent employment. It didn't say I had to have a certain level of job," Aiden replied, his brow furrowed. All the disadvantages he saw here were one thing, but if New Vancouver hid requirements, it would be even more upsetting.

"Well... I mean, they don't exactly do that, as far as I know. Send people away based on what work they have," Shuang admitted. "I just worry. Things aren't great. And you'll never make enough money here to finish out the same schooling you'd have in Subterra. Which is why I want to offer you a job with my family."

Aiden gestured for Shuang to sit. "What sort of job?"

"We run an accounting firm that works with the Subterrans who work in the fields. We do their taxes and run classes that teach them how to do taxes, all of that sort of stuff," Shuang explained. "I told my parents how quick you are at math and they said if you're willing to be trained, we could really use you."

"But don't you have machines and programs that can run the math for you?" he asked doubtfully.

Shuang folded her arms. "Our purpose isn't to make money. It's helping newcomers... like you. Quick, what's fifty-three times twenty-seven divided by twelve?"

Aiden rolled his eyes to the sky. Fifty-three times twenty-seven. That was... One thousand, four hundred, twenty-one.

So not a smooth division into twelve. He closed his eyes, visualizing the numbers in his head.

"One-hundred-nineteen, and a quarter. Point two five." He opened his eyes again.

Shuang was double-checking his answer against her palmheld and grinned. "See? You're a natural. We could pay you a lot more than you get working with Mama Bunting, and it would free up a space for her to take on an additional worker, too."

"She has space already; so far none of the other newcomers have applied." Aiden leaned back, frowning at the ground. "I only planned to be on the surface for a year."

On the other hand, what was his purpose under the surface? There was no need for accountants below the ground. He didn't want to spend his life doing nothing because he didn't have the freedom to move throughout the shelter.

Would it be so bad to make a life here on the surface? Maybe he'd be able to establish a solid, safe route to and from his old home, so he could visit them, or they could visit here.

He smiled as he imagined showing off New Vancouver to his family and Pat. While he didn't exactly feel like he 'fit in' here, at least he didn't 'stand out' the same way he had back home.

"I'll have to think about it," he said.

Shuang nodded, looking crestfallen. "Don't think too long, though. We have a lot of work... you see..." She hesitated, then took a deep break and plunged forward. "You see, my home bunker is failing. We're not the only ones, either. The technology is getting old and we're unable to collect the resources to replace it. It's happening all throughout the Subterranean settlements. We need to come back to the surface."

Aiden frowned at her, processing her words. Was this why she was so cagey when they were first making their way to the surface?

"My family came here to establish ourselves in New Vancouver, so we can help other Subterrans through the process of getting citizenship," Shuang continued. Her eyes creased anxiously at the corners. "We were also hoping to learn more about the New Vancouver terraforming equipment, so we might start forming our own settlements, too."

"And you haven't found anything?" Aiden asked, his frown deepening.

Shuang sighed. "Oh, we have the blueprints. They're free to whoever wants to see them. But it's the same problem as below the surface. How are we going to get the resources to make anything?"

"That is a problem," Aiden agreed.

"Which is why we're taking more steps, too," Shuang said. Her voice lowered as she glanced at the hostel doors. "We're going to demand that the Elders do something more. That they allow us to scavenge from Old Vancouver to get the supplies we need."

"I see." Aiden turned his gaze back to the sky.

"And we want Subterrans on the Elder Council, too. This city is run by Helians for Helians. How are we going to see any actual change if our voices are ignored?" Shuang sat straighter, her eyes fiery now. The determination twisting her face made Aiden's chest tighten.

He wasn't sure he liked the idea of making that sort of demand. Weren't the Elders elected to their position? While he understood demanding a new election in which Subterrans could run to be part of it, he wasn't sure about forcing the people to accept someone they didn't elect onto the council.

"Will you join us?" Shuang asked. "I understand if you don't want to."

"I'll have to know more about it... and give it some thought," Aiden said slowly. There was a lot to think about.

And a lot of his own research to be done as well.

THE PROTESTS STARTED the next day. Aiden kept a close eye on all the reports about the protests, making sure he understood exactly what they were doing. Mostly it was things like sitting in parks and singing traditional Subterran songs or marching in silence through the streets holding signs demanding their voices to be heard.

"It's absolutely disgraceful," Mama Bunting said a week later as she read the latest report.

Aiden looked up from where he was sweeping. His heart sank at her words. She was glaring at her palmheld, shoulders rigid, lips pursed.

"What is?" Ryn asked.

"That the Elders haven't so much as acknowledged the Subterrans yet," Mama Bunting replied. "Everything they're asking for is perfectly reasonable. Why can the Elders claim we don't have the resources for everyone, then turn around and refuse to allow newcomers to develop their own resources?"

Aiden let out a sigh of relief.

One of the Aerians sitting at the counter turned to Mama Bunting. "It's good to hear a Helian say that. So many don't understand what the issue is. But I tell you what, these Subterran protests are making us think about our issues, too."

Eira wandered closer to them. "What issues?"

The Aerian snorted. "Like how we're all stuck in hospitality jobs. I don't want to be in hospitality. I have training in welding, but nobody wants to hire me for it because of my thin arms. As though it takes massive amounts of strength to wield a two-pound tool."

"I like hospitality," Eira said.

Ryn leaned on the counter. "Then think about it as though it was a struggle to get into hospitality. Wouldn't that upset you?"

Eira nodded, her expression clouded.

The Aerian sipped their coffee. "We're going to have a meeting tonight to discuss the possibility of our own protest. Do you want to come?"

"Can I bring my friends?" Eira gestured at Aiden and Ryn.

"Sure. And you can come too, if you want," the Aerian said to Mama Bunting.

Mama Bunting shook her head. "Unfortunately, I can't. My daughter is going into hospital tonight and I promised to look after her baby. He's been quite sick and I can't risk taking him into a crowd."

The Aerian nodded. They finished up their coffee and then left. Seeing as they were the only ones in the café at this point of the day, it left the rest of them with nothing much to do. Aiden finished his sweeping quickly and Ryn mopped the floor after him.

With nothing left to do, Aiden made himself a cup of pepper and mint tea, made from ground white pepper and the mint grown in Mama Bunting's garden. He loved the combination of the heat from the pepper and the coolness of the mint. Ryn thought it was revolting while Eira settled for the more neutral, 'not to her tastes.'

"Mama Bunting, do you know why the Elders are so careful with resources?" Aiden asked once his tea was ready. "It seems to me like there is more than enough food here, and there could be many metals and other things scavenged from the old city."

"The old city is a graveyard. Remember, it's only been just over a hundred years since the cloud poisoned the surface," Mama Bunting explained. Her face twisted toward Old Vancouver. "I have great-grandparents who died there."

Aiden hadn't considered that before. His brow furrowed. How many lives were lost in the cloud? For that matter, what happened to the bodies? It was impossible that they would have been recovered and given proper burial rites.

Another thing to think about. How could they balance the solemnity of what happened there with the present need for the resources it could provide? And... and seeing as the Subterrans here were from fallout shelters so close to Old Vancouver, did they have an ancestral claim on the city, too?

He had a lot to think about, indeed.

AIDEN, Eira, and Ryn sat at the back of the meeting space. His hands rested lightly on his knees as he listened to Mr. Naiser, the Aerian leader, talk about what sort of provisions they wanted from the Elder Council. This was, apparently, based on a poll that had been spread through the Aerian community.

"What we feel is most disadvantageous is that we have been given specific places to live," Naiser said in a deep, rumbling voice that didn't quite fit with his petite frame. "We were promised integration into Helian society while maintaining our distinctions. It feels more as though we are judged on our distinctions. There is no integration—else why are there no Aerians at any levels of the government?"

Eira leaned in closer to Aiden. "I need to pay more attention to what's happening. I was only thinking about how easily I can breathe here."

Aiden squeezed her hand. It was understandable for her. She didn't face the same sort of things the rest of the Aerians did. Not yet, at least. Her life here must seem much more free than living in a single building for her whole life.

There was a slight commotion at the back of the room. Aiden turned to see Shuang slide into the room. She shifted from foot to foot, looking uncomfortable until she spotted him. Then she made a beeline and plopped into the seat beside him.

"Sorry I'm late," she muttered. "I got lost."

"That's fine," Aiden answered back.

Naiser cleared his throat. "As I was saying, we are starting a petition to bring more Aerians into the government—"

"Wait," Shuang exclaimed, jumping to her feet. "The Subterransare asking to be part of the government. Why are you trying to force us out?"

"We're not trying to force you out at all," Naiser said as the crowd muttered to each other.

"But we want to be part of the government," Shuang insisted.

Aiden winced. It was a good point. How much were the Elders willing to give the newcomers? If they were given positions, how could they then divide it up between Subterransand Aerians?

And Aquatics, he reminded himself as Ryn stood.

"May I speak?" Ryn asked, resting their hands on the front of the chair in front of them. "I know this is a meeting for Aerians and I'm an Aquatic but I think I have a few things that might be useful in the current discussion."

Shuang sank to her chair again. Her cheeks darkened, and she dropped her gaze to the floor, clearly upset at herself for her outburst.

Aiden gave her a small smile, but she didn't see it. Meanwhile,

Naiser had given Ryn his consent for her to take the podium, stating that he was eager to hear all the voices and that the Aquatics also had their issues with the Elders.

Ryn pressed their hands to the podium and Aiden was struck by how adult they looked. Even though they were a year younger than he was, they looked tall and confident. Their chin lifted as they gazed over the crowd, making eye contact with every single one of them.

"I think I know where things are going wrong," they started. "Because here in New Vancouver there is this idea that everything is limited. Food, resources, jobs, everything. But the thing is, there is no reason the council should be limited if new space is already being opened up. There is no limit to the amount of understanding and respect that can be given to everyone here."

Shuang let out a deep sigh, but her expression wasn't upset. Her brow furrowed in concentration and she leaned forward.

"They're right," Eira murmured to Aiden. "Everyone's been talking like if the Subterransget positions, then the Aerians can't."

Ryn twitched at the podium, the only sign of their nerves. "The Aquatics are also feeling restless. There's less of us here than Aerians and Subterrans. It's true, but from what I heard when I talk to others, we feel like we're invisible. But if we're all shouting different things at the same time, how will anyone hear us but ourselves?"

Naiser folded his arms, watching Ryn with a wary expression. "We know that this is a danger. But we are all tired of waiting to be heard."

"Then we need to shout the same thing at the same time," Ryn replied. "All of us— Subterrans, Aerians, and Aquatics—want the same thing. For our voices to be heard. So why are we keeping ourselves separate?"

Ryn looked out over the group, swallowed, and nodded. They stepped away and rushed back to their seat without another word.

Eira hugged them tightly. "You did good."

"You said that well, young Aquatic," Naiser said as he took the podium again. "If the Helians won't integrate us into their society, then Subterrans, Aerians, and Aquatics can integrate ourselves. We create a mosaic and then use our united voices to make the Elders listen."

Aiden sat straighter. He felt a shift in the room. He only hoped it was a shift toward better things... and that the Elders would listen to them.

10
UNHEARD VOICES

AIDEN WASN'T certain that this was the best idea. He was worried that protesting like this would end up being too aggressive to get a positive approach from the Elders.

On the other hand, the Subterrans had been trying to get their demands heard and nothing seemed to be working. It was only natural that they would try more extreme measures. He sat on a blanket on a small patch of clover, listening to the crooning voice of whoever was singing. It was a traditional lullaby, one that apparently had a similar tune but very different words to lullabies above the clouds and below the sea.

Beside him, Ryn's leg was bouncing. They were having a hard time sitting still.

"Relax," he told them. He had to close his eyes not to see the bouncing, but there were still tiny vibrations; it was getting so bad that he couldn't concentrate on anything else.

"I can't relax," Ryn muttered. "There's so much that needs to be done. I forgot to do my laundry yesterday. There's a new tea recipe I want to try. Oh, and—"

They cut off. Aiden opened his eyes to see that Eira had reached over to lay a hand on Ryn's knee. Her eyes sparkled as she shook her head.

"Remember, that's the point. There is a lot of work that needs to be done around the city, and we're showing just how vital we are for it. We as in the collective we." She gestured around.

Throughout the city center, the newcomers had set up blankets to sit on. Since the previous protests hadn't gotten the attention they wanted, they had escalated. Now, they were protesting in the city center itself. The Elders had to see the gathered people when they came to and from the Elder Council building.

Not only that, but the city had come to a halt. So many things, such as activating the robots that did daily work, or working in the fields, cleaning, and all the hospitalities were effectively shut down, not having workers in them. They weren't making any demands of the Elders right now; they were only gathered in this place to be seen. Subterrans, Aerians, and Aquatics all joined. They ate, read, listened to music, and told stories.

It was almost like a festival, but calmer than the celebrations Aiden was used to.

Ryn's leg started bouncing again. Clearly, they found it just a little bit painful to sit around and do nothing.

"Here, why don't you work on your text-to-speech program?" he suggested, digging into their shared pack. He claimed Ryn's palmheld and gave it to them.

They heaved out a sigh as they took it, crossing their legs. They hunched over the palmheld as they got to work on it. Aiden thought about correcting their posture, then decided he'd wait half an hour or so to give Ryn time to actually get into the work. If they were distracted too early, they would just toss the palmheld aside and go back to bouncing.

Eira shot him a grateful look behind Ryn's back, then took out her own palmheld. She made a note for herself and put it back, then stretched out on the blanket and closed her eyes.

How much longer would it take? Aiden didn't like how the Elders seemed to ignore everything, but then again, it was only the first day of this protest. Maybe they hadn't been aware of just how intense the discontent was among the newcomers of New Vancouver. He hoped that was it.

A little while later, a group of Helians walked up the pathway. Their faces were set in annoyed expressions as they looked around at the protestors. One of them looked at Aiden and his friends. It was the vendor, Mr. Julian, the vendor who refused to serve them. His lip lifted in a sneer at Aiden as their gazes met.

What was he doing here? Clearly, it wasn't to support the protest. A shiver ran down Aiden's spine as he looked away. Ryn was still absorbed in their palmheld and Eira's breathing was deeper now. Was Julian here to cause trouble?

The group of Helians passed by them, heading toward the Elder's council building. Aiden was glad that they didn't stop to say anything.

"What do you think sitting around on your butts is going to do, anyway?" Julian demanded.

Aiden sighed. He'd been relieved too early.

"Excuse me?" Shuang's voice rang through the air. She was supposed to be on the other side of the city center but must have come over to see them. "It's our right to have our voices heard."

Aiden scrambled to his feet as Eira sat up and Ryn straightened. Shuang had stepped in front of the group of Helians. For as tall and muscular as she was, she still looked dwarfed by the Helians. Julian stood nose-to-nose with her, but Aiden couldn't see his expression from this angle.

"Maybe instead of whining about everything we give you, work and be grateful we don't give your jobs to robots," Julian hissed.

Aiden slid between the Helians and took a spot next to Shuang. She bristled, her fists shaking as she glared at Julian.

"Thank you for seeing our side," Aiden said, keeping his voice even as he spoke.

Julian backed up half a step. "What?"

"Our jobs should go to the robots," Aiden continued pleasantly. "Seeing as there is more than enough technology to do all the manual labor that is instead put on Subterrans. We would be grateful indeed if that hard work was given to the more effective robots."

One of the Helians cocked their head forward, interested. "And then what would you do?"

"Well, if we didn't have to work so much, it would give us the time we need to pursue education and more enjoyable work. Creating art, for instance, or developing ways to make our underground societies more environmentally stable."

"So that's what this is about?" the Helian asked.

Julian snorted. "If you want education or whatnot, you should just do it. I work hard. Why should you get a free ride?"

"Why should you work hard if you don't find it fulfilling?" Shuang shot back.

Julian's mouth opened and closed. Then he folded his arms and scowled.

Aiden sighed. "I was sent to the surface with a year's worth of schoolwork and I haven't been able to complete even a week's worth yet, seeing as I have been working so much to meet residency requirements."

"You should be happy you're here at all," Julian said, coming at them from another angle.

The same Helian that had seemed interested before snorted. "It's hardly great luck that they've been forced out of their homes, Julian. Why should they be grateful to come to a place where they're promised a safe place to live, only to be forced into work they dislike?"

Julian threw his hands into the air. "We all have to do things we dislike! What makes them special?"

The Helians shook their head slowly. "Or maybe we should join in with our own demands for change. Isn't that why we're here? To submit a petition for the Elders to do something about those wolf rats?"

Julian glared at his companion and then pushed between Aiden and Shuang. The other Helians went around the two, although the last one tipped their head toward them.

"I'm sorry about that. Julian is... well. He's gone through a lot in his life. It's truly no excuse for his actions. I'll talk with him."

"Thanks," Aiden mumbled.

The Helian left. Aiden and Shuang went to the blanket, where they sank down. Aiden shook, so chugged back a bunch of water and stretched out on his back. Ryn set their handheld aside, chewing their lip as they looked up at the sky.

"Should we have come over?" Eira asked in a subdued voice. "I wanted to, but I was afraid I'd make it worse somehow."

Shuang took her hand and squeezed it. "I don't know. It would have gotten worse without Aiden, for sure. How do you do that?"

"How do I do what?"

"Be so calm?"

Aiden laughed dryly. "I'm used to bullies."

A heavy silence spread through the group until Ryn volunteered to teach them all an Aquatic song. Aiden closed his eyes, letting his breathing equalize again. This was serving a purpose. The Elders would hear them. They had to.

MAMA BUNTING HANDED AIDEN A SANDWICH, which he accepted gratefully. After a week of no movement from the Elders, not even an acknowledgment that the protest was happening, they stepped it up. Instead of staying on the grounds during the day, there were protestors here day and night.

Aiden, Ryn, and Eira were coming to the end of their protesting shift. They still needed to keep up their hours of work for residency, and so had went to work when they needed to, then came back after their shifts. It was exhausting and Aiden was tiring of sleeping on the ground, but what choice did they have? He wasn't even sure of what the next step would be.

"Are you three doing alright?" Mama Bunting asked, frowning at them.

Ryn yawned behind their hand. "It rained last night and that kept me up. But today is going to be better."

They had a lean-to shelter now, to keep both rain and sun off of them. It was a high-fiber blanket connected to poles on one side and staked to the ground on the other. Beneath it were the blankets and pillows that Yaella and Ayasha had given them to bring along.

"Maybe today we'll get official word from the Elders," Eira said.

Aiden rubbed the back of his sore neck. Tensions were rising among the protestors. They were all getting tired. More than that, there was quite a bit of anger growing toward the Elders. Even after the Helians had demanded something from the Elders, they remained absolutely silent.

"I'm afraid it's not going to work," Aiden admitted. Despite Eira's attempts to keep their spirits bolstered, today his were as damp as the sky. "Why hadn't they said anything? It seems like they're planning on just ignoring us until we fight among ourselves."

Or, a darker part of his said, they were waiting until all the newcomers violated the terms of their residency and were kicked out. The citizens had more rights, but what if the Elders were rolling out new laws that would put even them in a more precarious position?

Mama Bunting gave him a thermos of his favorite pepper and mint tea. "I know this is difficult, but you can't give up now. The Elders always move at a slower pace. You are making your point, though. Your voices will be heard."

Aiden smiled his thanks. Mama Bunting's reassurance didn't make everything better, but he felt less dreary now that he had food and a hot drink. She continued on, her walking legs moving behind her as she handed out more food and drinks to the other protestors.

After they had eaten, Ryn suggested that the three of them walk around a bit. Eira agreed eagerly, but Aiden caught the worried look she cast him. He agreed, not because he wanted to, but because it was better than sitting around doing nothing for another day.

It misted lightly, but rather than making him even more dreary, it seemed to revive Aiden's spirits. Or maybe it was the walk itself.

"Do you really think that this isn't working?" Eira asked after a bit.

"I think that it's not enough," Aiden admitted. "I think this is still a good idea, and that we need to stick out with it. Maybe we need to have something else besides it, though. I think we need to take steps to get the fresh materials that we need."

"Old Vancouver is right there," Ryn murmured.

Eira let out a shuddering sigh. "Yeah. And I don't know, but I think taking the materials our ancestors already collected and using them for further good is a tribute to them. You know? I know if I built a house, and it collapsed, I wouldn't want it to be left. Even if it killed me in the process. I'd want people to come and use what they could from it."

Aiden's stomach was unsettled by this. He wasn't sure that either Eira or Ryn really understood just what a graveyard was. Neither Aquatics nor Aerians buried their dead. They didn't understand how sacred a place like that could be.

"We're not the ones who died there, though," Aiden told them. "We don't know what they would have wanted... other than, they probably wanted to live."

Ryn and Eira both fell silent, bowing their heads.

Aiden sighed. He had been thinking about this himself but... "There are no simple answers, are there? It will do less damage to the earth if we scavenge the old cities, even though they are graveyards, rather than rip up mountains for it."

Eira squeezed his hand. "But it's still awful to think about."

"Yes. It is." He looked around at the people sitting under their shelters, huddling together against the rain as it grew harder.

Then he looked up at the building where the Elders were, dry and uncaring, in their sealed chambers. His heart constricted as his jaw set. All at once, his mind was made up... even though it made him sick to think about it.

"It is awful," he murmured. "But it's necessary."

11

OLD VANCOUVER

IT TOOK them a couple of days to find maps of Old Vancouver and make their plans to go to the city. Eira had more than a few moments of doubt as they made their plans. It felt wrong to decide to do this without consulting anyone else.

"We have to find out exactly what's there," Ryn argued late one night. "If we go, we can come back and tell everyone what we saw and if there are resources there at all. For all we know, there isn't anything that can be salvaged."

"When you put it like that..." Eira sighed as she shook her head. "I guess I'm just afraid of getting into trouble with the Elders. If we don't get citizenship, where will we go?"

Ryn and Aiden might live in the village on the top of the Cascade mountains. Maybe the lung-capacity adaptations would work on them, even if the adaptations they had previously tried wouldn't. But where would she go? Even the upper levels of Subterra would hold too much residual radiation for her.

Ryn grabbed her and stared determinedly into her eyes. "If the Elders kick us out, then we'll find a new place to live. We'll take seeds with us and go down the valley until we find a new spot of fertile ground. We'll make our own city."

Even though it was, of course, not realistic, Eira felt better once she heard that plan.

The fact was, they had to go. The Elders' silence was causing trouble. Some people in the protest thought that they were waiting out the protestors and the silence was a condemnation of them. Others who were against the protest thought that the Elders being silent was to support the protest.

Neither was right. The Elders were just being silent.

So here they were, heading into Old Vancouver.

Eira shivered as she looked at the century-old devastation. The land was barren, not even moss or grasses having reclaimed it yet. Everywhere she looked were rusted lumps and twisted shapes. Here and there a pane of glass gleamed, and it was only after they had gotten several meters into the city that she realized that the blobs of metal had once been buildings. She measured the length of one with her eyes, noting the way it wrapped around itself.

"Do you think they built them like this or...?" she asked, but stopped because her voice was too loud in the silence.

Ryn reached back to take her hand. "It really is a sobering sight, isn't it? No wonder the Elders who came before didn't want to take anything from this old city. Some of the original ones had to have lived here before... they could see just how much damage the cloud did."

"I don't know if we should be here," Eira murmured, giving voice to her doubts. "It really does seem like a graveyard. The air tastes wrong, too. What if the cloud is still here?"

"It can't be," Aiden said automatically, though his voice was doubtful. "Air doesn't work that way. This place has the same elevation as New Vancouver and there isn't a pressure system or anything here. If it wasn't safe, the Elders would say that outright, anyway."

That was true.

Ryn squeezed Eira's hand. "We're here for a reason. To find out what exactly is happening and how we can make things better for everyone else. Right?"

"Right," Eira murmured.

"Then let's go."

They set off cautiously, noting everything they saw. They quickly found that the outer edges of the old city were more barren than the inner parts. As they climbed through the twisted metal, they found lichen, moss, and more. Bird droppings and the skeletons of fish. As well as the hard, fist-size pellets of wolf rat droppings.

"Do you hear that?" Aiden asked, cocking his head.

Eira strained her ears, but all she heard was the wind. "Are there rats coming after us?"

Aiden turned to her in surprise. "No. The music."

"Music?" Eira and Ryn asked at the same time.

"You don't hear it?"

Both of them shook their heads. A furrow pinched Aiden's brows as he slowly shook his head from side to side. Eira could almost see his ears twitching. He started forward, concentration heavy on his face. Eira followed as quietly as she could, while Ryn took up the rear, keeping a careful eye on them.

After ten minutes, Eira could hear the music, too, though she had no clue where it was coming from. She trusted Aiden, though. Maybe, even though all the adaptations hadn't worked out for him, he still had a heightened sense of hearing from them, just like she had a heightened sense of the air around them.

Eventually, they came to a building that seemed to have suffered less damage than the others. It seemed to have compressed, rather than twisted and melted. They found an opening in the back and carefully squeezed in one by one.

Eira gasped. The roof was just over their heads, no doubt from the compression, but that wasn't what impressed her.

Books.

Hundreds of books! Her eyes widened as she held her hands out, as though trying to embrace them all. Her heart hammered. These were ancient, hundred-year-old books. During the Fallout, all the shelters had brought their books and knowledge with them digitally. There was no room for the physical copies.

"I've died and gone to heaven," she breathed as she bent to gingerly pick up the first book. It was heavy and brittle, and when she opened it the most terrible smell assaulted her nostrils. It choked her and made her gag.

She shut the book and put it back down. They needed a team to collect this and air them out before they could be read.

"Here," Aiden said, gesturing her over. Ryn was still near the entrance, peering outside suspiciously.

Aiden showed Eira something that looked like a palmheld, only it was about ten times the size and very bulky. Weird wires poked out from the back and when Eira touched the screen, it only crackled a little. This was where the music was coming from.

"What is it?" Aiden asked aloud.

"A computer!" Eira exclaimed. She smacked her forehead. "I've seen these in the old movies. Near the end, they were connected to a solar system. That must be why it still has power."

"Wow," Aiden murmured.

There were a handful of pamphlets scattered on the floor around the computer. She carefully picked one up, but it didn't spit poison air in her face like the book had. She brushed some crud off the top and peered at the words. It was about the Arctic drilling program, the one that had released the cloud.

"We need to get moving again," Ryn said.

Eira shook her head as she clutched the pamphlet to her chest. "I need to collect as many of these books as I can. Go on; just don't forget me before you head home."

Ryn looked uncertain, but Aiden nodded. They squirmed back outside and Eira found a clean spot on the floor and read.

"WE HAVE TO GO!"

Eira's heart jumped to her throat as she looked up. Aiden was crouched in the small opening, his face twisted with pain and urgency. Eira momentarily froze—there were so many books she wanted to bring!

"Now!" Aiden roared.

Eira shoved the pamphlets into her back, praying that they wouldn't get ruined, and raced for the exit. She shoved her pack through first, then climbed out. Aiden and Ryn grabbed her arms and hauled her through the rest of the way. Then they were running, one holding each of her arms still.

"What happened?" Eira demanded, struggling to keep moving forward at this speed. She felt like her feet were getting left behind and it was all she could do to keep hold of her pack.

She was answered by a series of eerie squeaks behind her. She turned once and caught sight of it—a wolf rat. The shadows seemed to dance around the wolf rat. Its elongated body was low to the ground, coarse fur covered in some sort of grime that she couldn't name. It scrambled forward with amazing speed, gaining on them.

Aiden grunted as he suddenly turned, releasing her. He grabbed up a piece of debris and bellowed, charging the creature. It jumped aside and reared back to its hind legs, screeching. Aiden threw the piece of debris toward it. The metal smacked it, eliciting another shriek.

Ryn turned and grabbed pieces of rusted metal off the ground and hurled them at the wolf rat. Eira drew herself up as big as she could, waving her pack over her head as she bellowed and yelled.

The wolf rat hissed, its coarse fur standing on end.

Then it suddenly turned and raced away. Eira stayed holding up her pack and roared again as the rat turned back once to look at them. Then it slipped between two bars of metal that seemed too thin for such a large creature. And it was gone.

Eira's heart pounded against her throat.

"Let's go," Aiden murmured. He put an arm protectively around Ryn.

They grimaced as they leaned against Aiden. It was only then that Eira saw a bandage wrapped around their leg. Blood was spotting the hastily made bandage.

"It surprised us," Ryn told her. "It grabbed me and tried to drag me away, but Aiden fought it off. We just have to get out of here. I'll be fine."

Eira nodded. She pulled her pack on and grabbed a long stick to use as a weapon in case they were attacked again. And she tried not to think about what would have happened if the wolf rat had found her alone, instead of Ryn and Aiden.

THE FIRST THING the trio did once they got back to New Vancouver was to get Ryn to the hospital. They needed several stitches and antibiotics, but the damage wasn't too bad. They got a doctor's easement for their working hours, too.

Back at the hostel, the three found a spot in the rec room away from the other teens staying in the hostel to discuss what they had discovered.

"The old government knew about the cloud for almost three years before it escaped," Eira said, laying the pamphlet out. It had miraculously escaped undamaged, and she had scanned it into her palmheld while they were at the hospital. "The fallout shelters were built by the wealthiest people, and then they allowed highly educated people to go with them."

"Only the wealthiest?" Ryn asked, their eyes wide with horror.

Aiden shuddered.

Eira nodded. "But what's most important is this. The government and these wealthy people set up caches of terraforming technology all over the place. Not just in Vancouver, but all across the country, to clean the air and seas and land. It was meant to clean up everything as the cloud extended."

"Why didn't it, then?" Aiden demanded.

"I don't know. The pamphlets don't say anything about that." Eira went through her palmheld and found what she was looking for. "But look at this. The terraforming tech that the Helians claim to have built? The specs are almost exactly the same. I'm not an engineer, but it's obvious, isn't it? They didn't build this technology, they used technology already put in place."

Ryn touched the pamphlet. "So... so only the Helians knew that this terraforming technology was here?"

"Maybe the Elders don't know about the caches," Aiden said. There was a doubtful gleam in his eyes.

"From what I can see, the Helians are the ones that held the codes to activate the terraforming caches," Eira said. "If they would activate all the caches, it would clear the poison left in the environment. We could all reclaim the surface. We'd all be free to live where we chose, instead of being regulated to under the ground or above the skies or in this city."

Ryn rubbed their eyes. "But they didn't activate it. Why didn't they? What happened?"

Eira's hands bunched into fists as she glared at the pamphlet. "What are they hiding?"

12

WANTING CHANGE

RYN WAS the one who volunteered to take a copy of the pamphlet to the leaders of the faction. The Aerian leader, Mr. Naiser, with his kind eyes and jovial smile, looked worried when he heard that the three of them went to Old Vancouver. The leader of the Subterraneans, Mx. Dawson, shook their head as their midnight-black hair quivered with their rage. Only the leader of the Aquatics, Miss Sevilen, didn't give any indication about what she thought of the whole affair.

"So you can see, there are more answers that the Elders have to give us," Ryn said as they clasped their hands behind their back. "Eira and Aiden searched all night but couldn't find anything about these caches in the network."

"This is grim," Naiser said, shaking his head. "What reason could the Elders have for hiding this?"

"They're hoarding the technology to themselves, to ensure the surface remains belonging to them," Dawson barked, bunching their fists.

Sevilen cleared her throat. "Or perhaps the Elders have tried to find and use these caches, only to discover that they didn't survive the cloud. It's not good to jump to conclusions."

"We should demand answers all the same," Naiser said as he slumped back. "Not that the Elders have told us anything of late."

The bitterness in his voice was all too clear. Ryn flinched as they rubbed their palms against their pants. They felt sweaty and cold for no reason. The wolf rat's bite hadn't left behind any infection and they had received good medical care. They would be in minor pain for a few days, but the attack hadn't been too bad—mostly the wolf rat had ruined their clothes.

They still felt odd.

"My friends and I will take a copy of the pamphlet to the Elders," they said before the adults could start arguing. "We can see their reaction and hopefully get some sort of official answer to it."

Naiser frowned uneasily. "I don't like the idea of involving kids in this."

Ryn couldn't help but scowl. Calling them 'kids' made them seem a lot younger than they were. "We all braved a perilous journey alone to get to the surface of the planet. We have nowhere else to go if the Elders decide to stop integrating newcomers entirely. We're already involved."

"They are the ones that got it in the first place," Dawson said.

Ryn nodded their thanks and looked back at Naiser and Sevilen. Truthfully, they were certain that even if the three leaders didn't give their consent, the three of them would go anyway. They had discussed this quite deeply the previous night.

In the end, Ryn would rather have their blessing so that everyone was working together. But if Naiser and Sevilen said no, Ryn would just have to tell them both that it was already decided. This was more of a courtesy than anything else.

Sevilen nodded. "You took the risk of finding this information. It's only right that you take it to the Elders. But remember, you weren't supposed to be there at all, so you will have to face the consequences."

"Thank you for the reminder," Ryn said.

"That's just it, though. They should not face those consequences on their own," Naiser argued.

Sevilen put her hand on his shoulder and squeezed lightly. The indifference on her face melted away, and Ryn wondered what the relationship was between them. While it was a simple touch, there seemed to be a tenderness in it that most people didn't share with acquaintances.

"They won't face it alone," Dawson said, straightening themself. "If they get in trouble for this, we'll stand behind them. It's not right for them to be censured for trying to help this city."

Ryn nodded their thanks again.

Naiser sighed. "Very well. I'll agree to this, then. Where is the original?"

"We're keeping it safe," Ryn said slowly. "We have the scans to share as well as copies that Aiden and Eira are making off the scans. We thought it might be best to keep the original tucked away for now."

It was with the painting of them on the ice.

"Good," Naiser said with a nod. "Be ready to produce it if necessary, but it's good to keep it safe."

Ryn bowed toward the three of them and headed out, their heart thudding. Back to the Elders it was. But this time the Elders would have to see that they had found the means to enact change, right? This time, things would be different.

How many more times could they hope the Elders would give the city what it needed, though? If this didn't work...

Ryn shook their head. It would work.

And if not?

Well. Change was coming, one way or another.

WHEN THEY GOT to the hostel to share the news with Eira and Aiden, they found Shuang there, too. Aiden and Shuang were nose-to-nose. While Aiden was about the same height as her, Shuang's muscular frame towered over him in sheer bulk. Her eyes flashed with anger as the two glared at each other.

"What's going on?" Ryn demanded as they hurried forward.

"They're arguing about what to do," Eira explained from where she stood nearby, wringing her hands.

Shuang let out a shaky snort. "We'll never be truly free if we don't take our freedom!"

"But what you're suggesting will lead to violence, Shuang," Aiden replied. His voice was firm and unyielding, like a storm wall. "I know you have suffered a lot more pain on the surface than I have. But please believe we are doing what we feel is best."

Shuang opened her mouth and shut it. She ran a hand through her hair, a frustrated expression on her face. "I didn't mean to."

Aiden sighed. "I know. I think maybe you should leave."

Shuang nodded. "Yeah. I think I should. Let me know what happens?"

"Of course." Aiden hugged her.

After Shuang left, Eira went to Aiden, touching his shoulder lightly. "Are you okay?"

"Yeah," he mumbled.

Ryn joined them. "What does Shuang want to do?"

"She wants to escalate the protests," Eria explained. "Instead of sitting, she wants to bar doors and going to the Elder's homes to chant outside their windows."

Aiden rubbed his forehead. "I understand where she's coming from—the Elders' silence is weighing on all of us."

Ryn grinned. "They won't be silent for long. We're going to the city center; we're going to get answers at last."

ELDER SUZANNE SLAPPED her hand on the table, interrupting Ryn as they were trying to tell the Elders about the pamphlet. "What were you doing in Old Vancouver? Have you no dignity at all?"

"We wanted answers," Eira replied, her voice quavering. "We thought maybe if we saw how Old Vancouver was, we'd know if there were old resources we could pull from it, rather than continually digging through the earth for new ones."

Suzanne's lips thinned.

"We thought it would be better to use what our ancestors already used, rather than damaging the planet looking for more," Aiden was quick to add.

"What makes you think you may disturb that sacred place?" Suzanne demanded.

Elder Francis rolled his eyes as he settled back in his chair. "Suzanne, I've been looking through the old records. Bunker 37, where Aiden is from, was filled with citizens of Old Vancouver just as Shelter Forty-Three A was. The Dome received applicants from around the world, but a good portion were from Vancouver as well. Aiden is for certain a descendant of Vancouver and has a claim. Ryn possibly has one."

"But the girl doesn't," Suzanne quickly said, as though desperate to find any way to make their actions beyond the pale.

Ryn struggled to keep their hands loose. Showing any sign of aggression, even if it was as simple as balling their fists, would be unwelcome in this environment.

"I haven't found information about Fata Morgana yet," Francis replied. "That doesn't mean Eira has no rights here."

Suzanne wrinkled her nose. "They stirred up the wolf rats that live in Old Vancouver. We've been getting more and more attacks—"

"Well, before these three went to the old city," another Elder interrupted.

They fell into arguing. When any of the trio tried to interrupt and bring the conversation back to what they found, the Elders simply ignored them. It was as though they had squabbled over these things that seemed inconsequential so as not to face up to what was really going on.

Ryn wasn't sure how much time had passed. It seemed like forever. Eventually, they'd had enough.

Shouting wouldn't do any good, though. It would only give the Elders something else to argue about. So they sat down, crossing their legs into a comfortable position, and sang. They closed their eyes as they did so, not wanting to see the expressions on the Elders' faces.

Ryn felt movement to either side, and then first Aiden's rich tenor and then Eira's high soprano joined them. The three sang in harmony, an old song that they'd discovered all three of them knew.

"Enough of this," Suzanne insisted. "They're clearly not interested in learning from their mistakes. Why should we—"

"We haven't even listened to them—" Francis argued.

Ryn sang a little louder, hoping to stop the Elders from this constant arguing. Their hands rested on their knees. The arguing grew louder as well, with Suzanne insisting that the trio be ousted while Francis kept telling her to stop talking and actually listen to someone else.

All at once, there was silence.

Ryn was startled out of their singing. Their eyes opened to find all the Elders staring in the same place. The oldest of the group, Elder Morgan, had stood up. Her snow-white hair was pulled back into a braid and her hands rested lightly on the table before her.

The silence swelled through the room until Ryn felt like nobody was even breathing.

"My mother, Elder Lindsey, was one of the first to leave the fallout shelters. She is the last among us with a living memory of what Old Vancouver used to be." Elder Megan paused, her gaze sweeping across the other Elders. "She would be the first to say we won't get anywhere talking over these children."

Ryn swallowed and got to their feet again, then helped their friends.

Elder Megan nodded to them as she sat.

It took Ryn a moment to fully understand what Elder Megan was saying. She was at least eighty, maybe even ninety years old. Her skin was thin and wrinkled, hands knobbed with arthritis. How much older would her mother have to be?

"They're children," Suzanne protested weakly.

"Our parents didn't spill their blood to build this society just for future generations to be scorned and ignored," Megan replied evenly. "Mx. Ryn, please continue."

Ryn threw their shoulders back, bolstered by this show of confidence in them. "Your parents brought you from below the surface. They followed dangerous paths to get here and build a place where you would all be safe."

Megan laid her knotted hands on the table. "They did."

"Well, we three all took dangerous paths, too. Only, we didn't have our parents with us to guide our way," Ryn said, their voice growing stronger. They started with their journey from below the ice, describing what they went through to get here.

Next, Eira took over and told her tale. She gave more detail than she had before, and Ryn found tears swimming in their eyes. Especially when Eira said that it was a one-way trip from Fata Morgana to the surface, and how she made this choice not because she wanted to, but because she had no other choice, and would likely never see her sisters or parents again.

Finally, Aiden told his tale. Rather than focusing on his trip to the surface, as the other two had, he described the painful procedures he'd gone through so that he could be adapted to the environment below the surface. He talked about the long recovery periods after each failed surgery and how each time he feared he might now survive it this time.

"I might be able to go back," he said slowly. "But to what? To a place I'm unable to live a full life. When I came here, I was filled with so much hope. That hope is dying day by day when I see the divisions here in New Vancouver."

"The foundation of your society is fractured," Ryn said.

"And that foundation can't hold the city," Eira added.

Ryn held up the copy of the pamphlet they found in Old Vancouver. "We want answers. About this. The terraforming caches that the old ones left behind for us."

Even Elder Francis looked unsettled by this. Ryn watched the faces of the Elders, trying to decipher what they were thinking. Unfortunately, other than the few like Suzanne who looked angry, none of them had their emotions on their faces.

So what could Ryn do to sway them? Something had to be done, but what?

Eira spoke again. "Does Fata Morgana know about the caches?"

No answer.

"Does Bunk 37 know?" Aiden asked. His voice was deeper and more rumbling than normal. Clearly, he was fighting some deep emotions.

Ryn squeezed his hand.

The Elders remained silent. This wasn't a good sign. Ryn frowned at them all, wondering why they wouldn't confirm or deny it. Some things were meant to be secret, but if that was the case, why wouldn't the Elders just tell the trio about it?

All of this silence only made Ryn's hackles rise. Not that they were angry—not yet at least—but it made them feel like they were somehow in danger. They didn't like not knowing what that danger came from.

"Our problems with the Dome came from our equipment wearing out," Ryn said, throwing back their shoulders. "And the equipment broke down and wore out far more quickly because of the acidity of the ocean. I could be safe at home right now if you had used the terraforming equipment more intensely to remove the remaining poison and acid from the ocean."

"Now, now, you don't know that," Francis said, his eyebrows pinching together.

"I do know that. There's no reason for the Dome to fail, unless it was eaten through by acid," Ryn shot back.

Suzanne shook her head. "You three don't know what you are suggesting."

Ryn looked at Elder Morgan, but she only sat silently, her face pulled in concentration. It appeared that, although she had stood up for them earlier, she wasn't going to do anything now.

"You need to share your knowledge of these caches with the city," Ryn insisted. Their hands tightened, the one still wrapped around Aiden's hand going white at the knuckles. "You need to tell everyone where they are. If we can get them started to be in use, it'll help everyone."

"And if they can't be used for whatever reason, then we can repair them," Eira suggested.

Aiden nodded his support. "It's not right to hold this technology back when it could do so much good. There was a Subterran family who tried to get residency at the same time as us, and they were rejected. They wanted to prevent their baby from having to undergo the adaptations for below the surface."

Elder Suzanne scoffed loudly. "That is their business. The city is set up as it is for a reason."

"New Vancouver could hold a higher population if you used the terraforming equipment," Aiden insisted. "I've looked at the math."

"That's enough," Suzanne said.

Ryn's throat constricted. The frustration and sense of danger had tipped them over—they were furious now. They wanted to yell but know that wouldn't do any good. They had to grind their teeth together to keep from making any noise. They didn't want to make the Elders angry.

"If you start spreading around these rumors of caches of terraforming equipment, it will do you no good," Suzanne continued.

"Rumors?" Ryn exploded, unable to stop themself.

Suzanne fixed them with a stern look. "Yes, rumors. You have no proof that this pamphlet is accurate. People before the cloud would make all sorts of promises to the people they never intended to keep. How will you feel if people go looking for these caches, only to wind up hurt or dead at their supposed location, with nothing to show for it?"

Megan spoke again at long last. "We will discuss this among ourselves. There is much that we have to take into account."

"The decision has already been made," Suzanne protested.

Ryn's shoulders slumped. They finally released Aiden's hand. It was clear to them that the Elders knew about the caches. Why were they so determined to pretend like they didn't? It seemed to be an impossible situation.

Francis sighed and shook his head. "You're confusing the children, Suzanne. We will discuss this information that they've brought to us."

"I... yes. We will discuss it," Suzanne grumbled. "But even if these caches are where you think they are, the power reserves needed to uncover them and get them to working condition will not be worth it."

And that was even more proof. Ryn lifted their chin. "We'll see."

The Elders all looked shocked, but Ryn didn't give them the satisfaction of being able to confuse them farther.

Instead, Ryn turned on their heel and marched out, Eira and Aiden following along behind. So the Elders would not do anything. They were too comfortable here in their city center. Which meant that the trio was going to have to do something. What, Ryn didn't know. But they would do something—no more sitting around waiting for someone else to solve the problems for them.

13

MAKING CHANGE

EIRA YAWNED as she stretched her arms over her head. A knot in her back made her grimace and she stood, doing some easy stretches to ease the pain. Now that her body was forcing her to move, that she realized how hungry she was—and that she needed to go to the bathroom.

She hurried to the bathroom, and when she returned, she found Ryn and Aiden at the table. They had both brought some food for her. Eira took it gratefully and devoured the soft rolls.

"Have you been doing this all day?" Ryn asked, sounding impressed.

"Yeah," Eira replied, around a mouthful of food. "When I get caught up in things, I sometimes forget about everything else."

She gazed at the table, filled with the project of her hard work. Having a copy of the pamphlet digitally was one thing, but Aiden had suggested they make physical copies as well. Eira had printed out hundreds of copies and had spent the day folding them to be easier to distribute.

Ryn and Aiden had been off today with Naiser and Dawson, trying to pull together a plan for how to distribute them... and what to do about the Elders. It had been a couple of days since the trio met with them. Since then, it'd been business as usual—silence. Eira was feeling even more annoyed and angry by it. Surely the Elders couldn't think that being silent about all of this was their best course of action?

"Did you figure anything out?" she asked hopefully.

Aiden shook his head as he sank into a chair. "Unfortunately, we can't decide on the best course of action. Naiser is adamant that we first make sure that the Elders know the city is getting the information before we make any demands."

"That's not going to work, they already know what we said," Ryn complained.

Eira tapped her chin. "But we didn't say what we were going to do. I think Naiser is right, to a point. We need to keep things open for the Elders to respond. We can't just put off plans for it, though. We need to make a major statement, one that can't be missed."

Ryn grabbed a carrot off the plate and munched on it.

"What do you suggest?" Aiden asked.

Eira laced her fingers together. "I read a story about a man way back in the ancient past. He was part of a religion and thought that things needed to change, so he wrote everything down and then nailed it to the door of the religion's holy building. I can't remember all the details, but I'm sure it worked."

"So you think we should nail it to a door?" Ryn asked.

"To the door of the Elder's building at the City Center," Eira said seriously. "If I know that story, they have to, as well. It will show how serious we are."

Ryn nodded. "Then I agree. Let's do that."

The two looked at Aiden, who seemed deep in thought. He traced the grain of the table for several seconds. When he looked up, his eyes were hard. "I can't think of a better way to do this. Let's go tell the others."

EIRA'S STOMACH twisted in on itself as she stood in front of the beautiful doors of the Elder's council building. Her palms were slick as she pressed the point of the nail into the wood. The hammer made an awful thudding noise as she drove the nail in. There was nothing that could undo that damage, now that she'd done it.

But this was so important! The Elders were causing damage, too, and they kept themselves so isolated from everyone else that they couldn't even see it.

This wasn't the only door getting a nail in it. The others were around the city, nailing copies of the pamphlets on the doors of other important buildings. This was their first step... it felt like outright revolution to Eira. An uprising against the Elders.

"Hey!" a crimson-clad guard came running over. "What are you doing?"

Eira took a deep breath. "My name is Miss. Eira, yours?"

"What?" the guard shook their head. "Mr. William."

"Pleased to meet you, Mr. William."

"Never mind that!" William stared, aghast, at the pamphlet nailed to the door. "What are you doing?" This is public property. You have damaged public property! Why? That's so rude!"

Eira swallowed hard. She didn't like being berated like this. Bracing herself, she handed over an extra pamphlet. The guard took it, looking too stunned to be angry. It was like he had no idea what to do when someone actually didn't listen to the societal rules.

"What is this?" William muttered.

"It explains what I'm doing here," Eira said, looking him in the eye. "The Elders have been keeping secrets from us all."

William's eyes widened. He opened the pamphlet and Eira marched away, trembling but certain. This had to be done. Now it was onto the next stop.

Eira kept having nightmares about evil guards showing up on the hostel doorstep to drag her away. She concluded that she had watched far too much television during her life cooped up on Fata Morgana. That sort of evil guard didn't exist here.

But even though the pamphlets had been distributed, and it was impossible for the Elders to not know what was going on... nothing. No word from them. No acknowledgement, no answers, nothing. Eira could understand if the Elders were divided in how to respond they might not want to say anything that would commit them to a certain path.

She couldn't imagine the reason for not even a 'we are aware of the situation and discussing a course of action' announcement.

"Here's your latte, sir," she said, handing a customer a cup.

The man nodded his thanks and left the café. They'd been so busy today that Eira had had little time to think about the current circumstances. But now they were at the end of the day and Mama Bunting locked the door.

And all of Eira's concerns and frustrations rushed in on her. She flopped her head onto her arms, groaning. It was bad enough that the day had left her physically exhausted.

"I feel like my head is going to explode," she complained.

Ryn patted her shoulder. "Because of work or...?"

"Because of 'or'," Eira replied grimly.

Aiden swept up. Ryn grabbed a cloth to wipe down the counter. Mama Bunting was already refilling the sugar.

With a groan, Eira went into the eating area and lifted chairs onto the tables.

"Maybe we're not doing enough," Ryn said sadly.

"You three are doing plenty," Mama Bunting replied soothingly. "You're working full time and fighting for change in your downtime. You're exhausting yourself. This shouldn't be your responsibility. You should be able to focus on getting yourselves into a stable situation and leave this work to the Helians."

There was an edge to her voice. Eira frowned, glancing over at her. Mama Bunting's expression was twisted in frustration. It seemed she already knew what they were all thinking.

Aiden was the one who said it out loud. "Too many Helians are comfortable with the way things are. They don't want it to change. So it's up to us, because we're the ones who are actually suffering with how things are."

Mama Bunting winced. She screwed the tops onto the sugar containers as she sighed. "You're right about that. And I'm sorry. It's not fair to you. It's not fair to anyone."

"Sometimes it's hard for them to see just how bad things are for other people, if they have a good life themselves," Aiden said with a shrug.

Eira put the last of the chairs up and went to Mama Bunting's side and hugged her tightly. She didn't like to see the friendly, cheerful woman so discouraged. "You're working to change things. You understand."

"Thank you. Sometimes I wonder if what I'm doing with Yaella and Ayasha isn't enough, though. Maybe if I was a bit braver—" Mama Bunting cut herself off and shook her head. "Well. Never mind about that. You three don't need to worry about me on top of everything else. Go ahead and head home early; I'll finish up around here."

"We can help," Eira protested.

"As your employer, I'm telling you to go home," Mama Bunting said in a playfully stern voice. "You've all gotten your hours for the week already."

Eira had to admit she loved the idea of getting back to the hostel. Maybe they could go to the pool this evening. She always found swimming incredibly relaxing, even if she struggled in water when her feet didn't touch the bottom.

EIRA SPLASHED SHUANG, who ducked under the water to come at her from behind with tickling fingers. Eira shrieked and pulled herself out of the water, hiding behind Aiden. Shuang, dark hair plastered to her head, surfaced once more. She was laughing, which was a rare thing to see these days.

"I wish we could do this all the time," Eira said as she jumped back into the water. She paddled around, the physical exhaustion from the day having disappeared with the fun.

Shuang grabbed Ryn's hands and pulled them into the water. "We could, if the Elders..."

Eira scowled. She didn't want to talk about them again!

"I was thinking about what you told me," Shuang said as she came to a stop, her expression growing serious. "How Elder Suzanne said you have no proof? Well, I was thinking we should find proof. There's a cache over on Vancouver Island. If we can get there and prove that it works, the Elders won't have any excuses anymore."

"Will it?" Ryn said doubtfully. "I'm not sure they care about excuses, honestly."

"We can try," Eira said doubtfully. She chewed her lip. But was it safe?

Shuang read her expression correctly. "We'll bring with us some emitters that drive away the wolf rats."

Eira glanced at Aiden. He'd been quiet through all of this, and she wanted to know what his thoughts on the issue was. He was deep in thought as he paddled his feet in the pool. It seemed like he was going through a lot of thoughts before he finally looked up again.

"I agree with Shuang. We need to find the equipment and see for ourselves if it works or not," he said slowly. But his gaze was still worried. "We have to be careful, though. The cache is on Vancouver Island, which is through Old Vancouver and across the strait."

"I know where we can get a boat," Shuang answered.

Aiden nodded once. "I haven't had the time to study since the sitting protests and I know I'm not suited for jobs requiring a lot of physical labor. I don't like that my options seem to be limited to going back below the surface where I'm in constant danger, just so I can finish my education, or stay here and work so hard I won't have time for it."

A grimness fell over the four teens, Eira looked at her friends, studying each one. They were all lost in their thoughts. Shuang had clouds behind her eyes, as though she was remembering something that was too painful to share. Eira reached out to her. Shuang first shied away from the touch, then sighed and accepted her hand.

"It feels strange," Shuang murmured. "I came here intending to convince you three to do this. But not that you've agreed... I can't help but wonder if it's wrong. If I'm being too hasty and I've, I dunno, infected you with my impatience or something."

"You haven't infected me," Ryn assured her. "My patience was already wearing thin. It makes sense for us to go see for ourselves."

Eira nodded, though she understood where Shuang was coming from. The idea of crossing the strait and digging up an old terraforming cache was intimidating. How much could the four of them really do? They didn't even know what was on Vancouver Island.

But it was necessary. They had to show everyone that the tech still worked. And if it didn't, then they needed to tell everyone that they had made a mistake. Either way, something had to be done.

They got out of the pool and headed into the change rooms to dry off and get dressed. As she toweled off her hair, Eira thought about the Elders again—and formulated a letter in her head. She'd write to them, begging them to think about their history and how the terraforming equipment could prevent their pasts from repeating.

With this tech, nobody would ever have to go hungry again. And wasn't that something they all wanted?

SHUANG BROUGHT along a pair of walking legs on their trip. They loaded it up with the emitters to keep the wolf rats away, as well as the other equipment they thought they would need. It was the weekend and so the trio had two days off from Mama Bunting's café. They had decided that they couldn't let anyone else know what was going on to protect them if this ended up putting them into trouble.

The trip around Old Vancouver to get to the sea was quiet. But once Eira saw the ocean, she gasped.

"It's beautiful!"

They stopped near the seaside. Shuang knew of a boat around here somewhere, but Eira couldn't tear her eyes away from the sea to help look. The water stretched out as far as she could see. It was a deep turquoise blue, even more beautiful in real life than the images she'd seen in videos.

Beside her, Aiden tucked his hands behind his back and looked out with an awed expression.

"You two are acting like you've never seen an ocean before," Ryn laughed.

"I haven't," both Aiden and Eira said at the same time.

Ryn joined them quietly on one side, with Shuang on their other side.

"So you lived in the ocean?" Eira murmured.

Ryn nodded. "Where I came up from the Dome, it was all ice. I had to punch through to get out. But this is all melted, isn't it?"

"You must have been farther north," Shuang said. She shrugged and headed down the beach. "Come on. The boat's this way."

Eira followed slowly, her eyes still on that magnificent sight. But even as she did so, she could smell the sickly scent coming off the ocean. It smelled as though the sea itself was ill. Her heart clenched.

That's why we're doing this. Because we need to heal the Earth. This will work. It has to.

The boat ride was rough and took the rest of the day. They camped that night and, after a restless sleep, got up early to continue their search. They found the location where it was close to noon. To

Eira's relief and amazement, the hatch leading to the buried equipment was still intact. The acid rains had welded it shut, but they could cut it open thanks to the equipment Shuang brought.

Shuang led the way down into the Earth. She carried with her a lantern that lit their way, but there were several times that she saw things that the others. They placed the emitters—small, circular speakers that played a high-pitched squeal—every few meters. The sound obviously bothered Shuang and Aiden more than Eira and Ryn.

Eira didn't like the feeling of being below the surface. This was far different from the pocket of the library that they had found in Old Vancouver. It closed in around her and even though the space was fairly large; she felt as though she couldn't breathe.

"What if the cloud got trapped in the air down here?" she asked, loosening her collar.

"It couldn't have," Aiden replied. "Look at these stairs; they're metal and are in perfect condition. The cloud would have melted them."

He was right, but it didn't comfort Eira at all. She tried to ignore the twisting of her stomach, knowing that all of what she was feeling was just in her head. There was no danger down here. But she eyed the ceiling warily. Now that Aiden pointed out how structurally sound the stairs were, she was worried about that metal roof. Were there buckles in the metal, or was that all in her imagination?

They came to the terraforming machine suddenly. The stairs ended and a long, shiny machine stood at the end of them. Shuang lifted her lantern, but none of them could get a good look at it.

"It looks a bit like the tunnelers," Aiden said, squinting. "They go through the surface of the earth looking for deposits that we need to mine."

"It looks like an underwater craft," Ryn said.

Eira found a plague on the wall and called them over. Shuang lifted the lantern and Eira read aloud.

"The Whale was designed to travel through the ocean filtering out toxins as it comes in contract with them. It is a manned vehicle and can clean up to two thousand gallons per hour. It contains an internal engine that produces electricity to power itself as it goes through the water but must be charged every week in the sunlight."

Ryn tapped their chin. "So how do we know if it works, if it needs to be charged by sunlight?"

They returned to the vessel and looked over it. On closer inspection, it was long and conical, like the body of ancient sharks. It had a dorsal and pectoral fins for its stability, but rather than a tail it had a port that shot water out of it. All over the metal body were small openings that would suck the water in.

Eira thought it looked very impressive, but that still didn't answer their question.

"Look." Shuang held up the lantern at the nose of the Whale. "There are some doors here. I bet they built a passage that goes straight out to the sea."

"Will it be able to withstand the acidity?" Aiden asked doubtfully.

Ryn leaned over the top of it and worked their fingers over what seemed to be a smooth shell. "We don't need to have all the answers. Just knowing that it's here is a big deal. It's not even anywhere near Old Vancouver, so if we can bring it back to New Vancouver, we'll be able to reverse engineer it."

They let out a cry of triumph when a panel suddenly slid back. They grinned as they leaned into the vessel.

"That's what I thought," they crowed as the other three drew closer.

"What?" Eira asked impatiently.

"These controls are the same as the watercraft I'm used to," Ryn explained. They slipped in and settled into the seat. "Comfortable. Now, if the engine works, it'll be—"

They flipped a switch. A rumbling filled cavern. Eira jumped, shrieking, but the others laughed. Shuang's eyes glowed with excitement while Aiden looked on with a satisfied smile. Eira got her pounding heart back under control and smiled, too. It worked! Which meant the Elders had no more excuses.

Ryn flipped the switch back down—the rumbling continued. Alarm swept over their face as they flicked it up and down.

"It's not turning off," they cried.

The ground trembled beneath their feet. Aiden and Shuang, used to these slight tremors, ignored it as they tried to help Ryn.

But Eira felt it. And she saw the way the stairs were shaking. The way the buckles she thought she had imagined on the roof grew deeper. She grabbed Aiden's arm.

"We have to get out of here!" she cried in alarm.

It was too late. With a screeching sound of broken metal, the roof collapsed and thousands of pounds of earth poured in on them.

RYN COUGHED on the dust in the air as they climbed out of the Whale and stumbled toward the light Shuang still held. Trickles of dirt and rock still streamed from the opening in the ceiling, but it seemed as though the worst of it had ended.

The bad news was the entrance was completely blocked.

"Is anyone hurt?" Aiden asked, pulling first Ryn, then Eira into the light so he could check over them. Shuang had a slight cut above her eye, but other than that, they didn't seem to have been hurt.

"I thought I was going to be crushed," Eira said. Tears streamed down her face, despite her obvious attempts to keep herself collected. "I thought that—but Shuang pulled me away just in time. Thank you."

She clasped her hands over her heart as she bowed her head to Shuang, who shrugged.

"Don't think anything of it. You'd have done the same for me." She looked embarrassed, but she smiled, pleased with the praise.

Ryn viewed the pile of collapsed earth. It stank terribly, much like that sickly smell that had been running off the ocean. No doubt this was filled with toxins, too. "I bet what happened is that when the rains were acid, it soaked so deep into the earth that it compromised the ceiling. Then when I turned on the machine, the vibrations made them crack."

Aiden nodded. "I agree. That is the most likely thing that happened. At least the Whale is off now."

"Yeah. It shut off by itself." Ryn shrugged. The batteries must have run out.

"What do we do now?" Eira asked in a subdued voice. "Can we dig out?"

Shuang hummed as she inspected the pile of dirt. "I wouldn't suggest we disturb this until we figure out a way to reinforce the ceiling. We don't want to move it just for more to fall in. We might not be so lucky next time."

Aiden nodded.

Ryn sat on the nose of the Whale. "In the meantime, let's all just take a minute to sit down and breathe, okay? That was a close call, and we need to clear our heads."

Eira groaned as she sank down next to Ryn. Aiden joined them as well, but Shuang kept walking around the pile, peering at it from every angle. Ryn closed their eyes and leaned back, trying to catch a bit of rest. Every bone in their body felt tired.

Shuang let out a strangled, triumphant cry.

"What?" Eira asked, sounding frightened.

"I think I have an idea. We don't have to move the whole pile of dirt. We just need to get to the entrance, right?" Shuang continued without giving them the chance to answer. "So we can dig down from this side here," she said, pointing, "and we can use these fallen rocks here to build up a wall around where we're digging to build up a retainer wall. We'll have to go one at a time, but we can do this."

She hurried down to where the rocks were and poked through them.

Ryn headed over. "I'll go first with the digging while you get the best rocks."

"Good," Shuang said distractedly.

Eira made a noise in her throat. "What should Aiden and I do in the meantime, then?"

Aiden answers. "Let's take as many scans of this machine as we can on our palmhelds, so we can bring back information to New Vancouver."

Ryn grinned as they all started their work. They might have suffered a setback, but they'd get out of here. All they had to do was work together.

IT WAS nighttime before the four of them emerged from below the surface. They were all filthy and exhausted. Their eyes and lungs stung from all the toxic dust, and Ryn worried about the long-term effects this might have on them.

As they were setting up camp, though, a light emerged in the darkness. It hovered in the sky, swinging back and forth for some time. Ryn watched it, trying to figure out what it was.

"What is that?" they asked, pointing.

The other three turned. Eira and Aiden both frowned, puzzled, but Shuang whooped.

"It's a search party! We need light. They'll see where we are!" She grabbed the lantern and jumped on top of the walking legs, waving the light over her head.

The searching light drew nearer, along with a strange chopping noise. Wind gusted over them as the light landed on their little spot. It blinded Aiden, and he threw a hand over his face, squinting against the brightness.

The machine, which was a bulbous thing with a fan on the top that apparently provided lift, landed further away. A group of adults, Naiser among them, jumped out of the machine and ran over to the teenagers.

When Shuang explained what happened, the adults sprang into

action. They set up four stalls for the four of them to wash the dirt off their bodies, with the promise that they'd go straight to the hospital afterward to make sure they were alright.

As they cleaned up, Ryn asked Naiser how he knew where to find them.

"Yaella and Ayasha were worried that you hadn't been to the hostel, and so reported you being missing. When nobody heard anything from you, the Elders authorized search parties. They figured you were heading here."

Ryn sighed. Well, at least they had kicked up enough of a fuss in New Vancouver that their whereabout would be known. They didn't like the idea of having to make their way back to the city on their own.

"Are we in trouble?" Eira asked, her voice shaking.

Naiser sighed. "I don't know. I suppose that will be up to the Elders to let you know one way or another."

MORE WAITING.

It had been three days since the Ryn and her friends had found the Whale. They reported everything that they had discovered to the Elders... and so far; the Elders had said that they weren't allowed to leave the city and each of them were given a bracelet to track their locations.

Their place as residents was, currently, not in jeopardy because of the special circumstances of their arrival. All except Shuang, who was told in no uncertain terms she had to keep her nose clean or else she would be sent back below the surface.

That should have been enough, right?

It wasn't, apparently. Ryn felt as though the customers at the café were constantly giving them dirty looks. Worse, one night when they were heading back to the hostel after extra-long shifts, the cake vendor, Mr. Julian, confronted them himself.

Julian waved the pamphlet they had distributed about the caches of terraforming equipment in their faces. "What do you think you are doing?"

Ryn scowled and stepped back. "What are you talking about?"

"This is you, isn't it?" Julian demanded. "Spreading all of this unrest. Isn't it good enough that you're here? That you're taking resources that should go to Helians, and instead you're causing all this trouble because you don't want to work hard?"

Eira pushed his hand away. "We're already working hard. The problem is that outsiders are forced into a narrow range of jobs that—"

Ryn interrupted. There was no point in arguing that. "What resources?"

"What?" Julian said, turning to them.

"What resources are we taking? We have tried to give you money, and you refused it. What resources do you not have because we're here? You're a Helian, you have free education. We don't. But if more people had education, then there would be more educators, so there wouldn't be a shortage."

Julian scoffed and shook his head. "It's not about the education."

Ryn threw their hands into the air. "Then what is it about? Please, tell us! How are we making your life more difficult?"

"You all come from cushy settlements. You never knew what it's like to live with food shortages, to have lotteries drawn, to decide who gets enough food and who goes hungry for the week," Julian ranted, his hands bunched into fists. "You'll never know what it's like to starve!"

Ryn peered intently at him, the pieces finally clicking together. "You do?"

He glared at them.

He did. So what did that mean? Ryn wasn't sure. They hadn't

read enough about what it was like for the first Helians. Maybe that would have to change.

They folded their arms, frowning. What was the reason behind all the rules that the Elders put into place?

Maybe there was more to this story than they realized.

"THERE'S food all over the place," Eira said, gesturing around them. "Every building is crawling in fruit and vegetables. The robots are constantly harvesting. There's more than enough food."

Julian folded his arms, glaring at them. "My parents and grandparents didn't work themselves to the bone for decades under a harsh, unyielding sun, risking illness every time they worked in a new plot of land, just for kids like you to be ungrateful for what you have."

Aiden shook his head, unhappy, while Ryn looked on with a deepening frown.

Eira, however, reached over to touch both their hands, to indicate they shouldn't respond yet. There was something about the way Julian spoke that made her think that this wasn't as straightforward as they thought. She wished she knew why he was being so angry with them, but she supposed that if he felt like they were being unreasonable, he'd only be unreasonable in return.

"Why did your parents risk illness working with a new plot?" she asked. "Is it because the toxins from the cloud were still lingering in the soil, despite the terraforming equipment that was used?"

"The terraforming equipment had to be shut down for several years, because it was only causing a buildup of the toxins in other areas," Julian told her. "We had to use other means of eliminating it from the ground. I'm surprised you don't know that, since you want to live here."

Eira shook her head, understanding a little bit better. "I'm sorry that you and they went through that. But that's not what is happening anymore. If you look at the reports of crop yields, New Vancouver is producing enough food to feed a population ten times its current size."

Beside her, Aiden nodded. "And, you have to remember that we are struggling to put in the hours of work that are required for our residency. None of us have finished our schooling and we're trying to keep up with that, too."

"Why waste your time with this?" Julian brandished the pamphlet at them.

"Why are you so aggressive about it?" Ryn demanded. They put their hands on their hips and their eyes flashed. "We want to restore the world to what it was. Fata Morgana has the technology to restore entire ecosystems, but they can't because the vase majority of our planet is still toxic. How is it ungrateful or wasteful to want to make a world where we all have a place to be?"

Julian spluttered for a moment, but Eira thought maybe he was softening. If he was, he was determined to hide it. He spun on his heel and marched away, grumbling under his breath about trouble-makers and 'what is this city coming to'?

With an ironic glance at her friends, Eira continued. They got through the market quickly, but the closer they got to the hostel, the more Ryn's feet dragged.

"What's wrong?" Eira asked them.

"Did we do the right thing?" Ryn worried out loud. Their eyebrows drew in together and their shoulders slumped forward.

Aiden put an arm around their shoulders. "What do you mean?"

"I mean, it seems like there's only been an increase in the tension in the city since we released those pamphlets. I'm thinking that we moved too quickly. That we should have planned things out better." They lifted their wrist, where the tracking bracelet hung. "We wouldn't have these if we had."

"Maybe," Eira murmured.

"On the other hand," Ryn continued with a sigh, "I know that things just can't stay how they have been going. I'm just so mixed up and confused."

Aiden laughed as he patted their shoulder. "Yeah, I know. It would be a lot easier to ignore it all and hope that everyone else can have it figured out before it affects us personally."

"Exactly," Ryn said, shrugging. "I just don't know what we're supposed to do anymore. I really don't want to risk making things worse. On the one hand, we have people like Shuang who are desperate for change right now. Then, on the other hand, we have people like Julian who think this is just upsetting a careful balance."

They shook their head and sighed.

Eira was silent as they got back to the hostel. Her mind wasn't quiet, though, and she continually ran over the various avenues they had already taken to get some change. They hadn't given any sort of official report to the Elders about what they found on Vancouver Island. While it was safe enough to assume that the Elders had gotten a report from their rescuers, maybe they needed to keep going with their direct action.

When they got back to the hostel, she dug out the letter she had written to the Elders, but never sent. She showed it to her friends.

"We could write up what we found, and deliver it as a letter to the Elders," she suggested. "I'm just not sure if we should make it an open letter or not."

Aiden frowned.

"I'm not sure an open letter will do anything but cause more trouble," Eira said.

Ryn shook their head. "On the other hand, the people deserve to know what we found."

"We'll do both," Aiden said. "One, we'll write a letter to the Elders describing what we found and asking for an explanation as to their silence if change isn't possible. And another one, an open letter in which we tell the city why we're doing what we are doing and telling them we have found proof that the terraforming caches might be salvageable."

Eira beamed at her friend. Now that he said it, it sounded so reasonable, the perfect solution to their problems. She pulled out her palmheld and grabbed a stylus.

The three gathered together and planned out their letters.

THE LEADERS of the three factions stood at the front of the room, looking over the gathered group of Subterrans, Aerians, and Aquatics. Eira, Ryn, and Aiden sat with Shuang near the front of the room. All four of them were tense and quiet as they listened to the debate happening. Electricity charged the room; it was decided that tonight, the various leaders would present different plans as to what their next actions could be.

After that, there would be a vote. Then they would all know what collective action they would do next.

The Subterran leader, Dawson, leaned against the podium, their head lifted and their chin jutting out in defiance. "We have waited long enough for the Elders to do something. It's time we took action into our own hands and go in search of these caches ourselves."

Sevilen shook her head her gills lightly flapping as she did so. "We need to inform the Elders of this before we take such action. We need to have another sit-in, with the clear message of once it's done, we will go after the equipment."

As an answer, Dawson folded their arms. "That will take too long. How many chances do we give the Elders?"

Eira leaned forward slightly, her eyes on Naiser. So far, he hadn't said anything, and she longed to know what stance he was taking. There were so many conflicting thoughts in her head. She felt like they had been more than patient with the Elders, but at the same time if they only antagonized them, how would they ever have a place among the Helians?

"Perhaps instead we need to leave New Vancouver," Naiser said softly. "We could collect our things and journey to the southmost part of the cleaned land and start a new city there."

Murmurs broke out all around them. Eira's stomach cramped at hearing those words. She shook her head as she got up. The room was so crowded nobody took notice of her as she slipped outside. Maybe it was best, but starting over yet again felt even more difficult than the decision to leave Fata Morgana.

She needed air. Her lungs felt too small.

Once she was outside, Eira found a spot on the side of the building which wasn't covered in vines and leaned against it with her eyes closed. The air out here was cold compared to the room, but she knew that wasn't why she had shivered.

She heard footsteps drawing near and, inhaling deeply, found the earthy and salty scents of Aiden and Ryn. She didn't open her eyes.

"I feel like we're just spinning our wheels in the mud," Aiden said.

"What does that mean?" Eira asked.

Aiden sighed, leaning against the wall against her. "When a wheel gets stuck in mud, it spins and spins but can't get any traction to move, so it ends up sinking deeper while flinging mud everywhere."

That felt like an apt description of what they were doing.

"I just don't get it," Ryn said. "It's like we have two councils, but one is refusing to talk and the other doesn't have any power at all."

Eira's eyes opened. Of course. She straightened up. "I've been reading about the history of New Vancouver," she blurted.

The other two gave her puzzled looks.

"That isn't new," Aiden said.

Eira rubbed her hands together. Despite her new excitement, she was getting quite cold out here. Her floaty robes—the clothes she wore while leaving Fata Morgana—didn't do much to keep her warm. They were designed to reflect UV rays, not keep the body beneath warm.

"No, you see, back before the Helians left their fallout shelter, they were facing serious unrest," she explained. "In the end, the younger generations said that the Elders weren't adapting to their current circumstances and so they formed their own council. Then, when the previous Elders were lost, the new council was renamed the Elder Council. And people were voted onto it. As time went on, only older people were voted onto the council because of their wisdom."

Understanding dawned in Ryn's eyes. "And now the Elders are doing the same thing. They're not adapting."

"So we need to revive that second council," Aiden murmured.

Eira nodded, standing straighter. "One that will take action as needed."

Ryn grabbed her hand. "Let's get back inside and tell everyone this idea. Maybe if we have a second council, the Elders will finally act!"

They seized Aiden's hand as well and dragged the two back in. Eira's heart thudded as the three of them interrupted the debate and declared that they had another option, one that hadn't been discussed yet. She desperately hoped that this would work. Because if it didn't... well, she didn't know what was going to happen.

But things couldn't stay the way they were. The push and pull were both too strong; how long before everything broke?

THE NEXT DAY, there was another protest at the city center. This time, however, rather than peacefully sitting and hoping that the Elders would finally take notice as to what was going on in their city, the protestors made noise. They had chants; they waved signs, they continually kept it up.

"The Elders can't continue to ignore this," Eira said. Her arms ached from holding up her sign for hours now. She glanced up at the words.

Hear my voice!

Things hadn't gone the way she wanted the previous night. Rather than deciding to form their own council and then use their collective voices to demand acknowledgement from the Elders, half the people voted for the Elders to step down, and half of the others thought they should demand a new election including residents rather than just citizens. It was only a quarter that believed a new council alongside the Elders would work.

"How are we meant to be united when we don't have the same ideas what needs to be done?" she grumbled, marching alongside Aiden and Ryn around the Elder's building. The letters that they had sent to them had been returned unopened.

Eira thought it was about time for them to blast these letters around the same way they did the pamphlets but Aiden talked her down from that. They had misaddressed the envelopes; so they'd try once more, delivering the letters directly to the Elder's council building.

They had dropped them off this morning, but judging by the piles of letters in the boxes, it was gong to be a miracle for the Elders to see their letters.

The doors of the building, usually open, were locked. Nobody was allowed in. The guards told people it was for the Elder's health.

Eira understood what that meant. They were afraid someone would try to harm the Elders.

Hear my voice. She read again and tears blurred her vision.

"It's not enough," she whispered. "They'll never hear us. Not so long as they remain certain that they're doing the right thing."

Just as we're not hearing them; but at least we're trying to talk. They're just staying so silent!

She shook her head and gripped the sign tighter. They would figure this out. They'd get the change that New Vancouver needed. The Elders would see what needed to be done.

They had to.

15

A NEW ORDER

THE NEXT FEW days went by in a blur for Aiden. There was always something happening, whether it be officials coming to Mama Bunting's café shop to ensure that the three were actually working and not just sitting around; to their bracelets finally being removed; to rumors circulating that Fata Morgana was going to come and hover above New Vancouver and block out the sun.

Aiden felt as though he had no time to just sit and think. It was exhausting, always having to decide without the space to think about the consequences of his actions.

The next sit-in at the city center, he stretched out under the lean-to that he, Ryn, and Eira made. It was a miserable day, drizzling rain. The dampness pervaded everything, even the flannel blanket on the ground.

"You're going to get cold," Eira complained, her arms wrapped around herself. Her petite frame shivered, showing she was the cold one.

"I'm tired," Aiden told her, closing his eyes.

Ryn nudged him with their foot. "Naiser is standing up on the council building steps."

Aiden pushed himself back up, watching with eager eyes. What

had the three leaders of the factions have decided to do? Was there
going to be a vote?

"Friends," Naiser started in his deep voice, "we have gathered
here yet again to plead with the Elders to hear us. And yet they
remain silent, deaf to our calls. And so it is that we will now have to
take matters in our own hands, so our voices will no longer be
ignored."

A slither of doubt ran down Aiden's spine. What did he mean by
that? It sounded... ominous.

"And so we will form our own council," Naiser declared. "A new
authority in this city that will take our cries to the Elders themselves
and sit with them, a second layer of government. For too long the
Elders have had unmitigated power over our lives, while we never
were permitted a place among them. No more."

Aiden's shoulders slumped forward. "When was this decided? I
thought we were still going to discuss it... have a vote."

"Why would you think that?" Ryn asked, their brow puckered.
"The Elders have been ignoring us like tantruming children. We had
to do something."

"I know. I just... I guess I thought we'd have more time," Aiden
murmured.

He leaned his head into his hands, trying to figure out how long it
had been since that last meeting, when Ryn brought the suggestion to
the faction. Everything seemed like a blur, but it couldn't be more
than a couple of days.

"Hey." Eira put a hand on his shoulder. "Are you feeling okay?"

"Not really."

"Do you need to head back home?" she asked.

Aiden shook his head, but her choice of words stuck him. Was
the hostel really 'home'? The three of them still needed to find
permanent addresses. The hostel wouldn't provide enough housing
to be granted citizenship. And they'd been so distracted by everything else, they hadn't been looking for anything.

The hostel was the place they lived. They kept their meagre

belongings and slept there. It kept them warm at night and safe from storms. But was it home?

I'm homeless, he thought, his heart sinking.

Going back under the ground wouldn't feel like going home. It would feel like giving up. Tears pricked his eyes. He wanted so badly to see his parents and Pat. He wanted for all of this to be over, so he could focus on his studies and make something of himself that his parents could be truly proud of.

Eira put an arm around him and leaned against his side, though Aiden wasn't sure if that was because she was offering comfort or seeking warmth.

"Do you need to talk about it?" Ryn asked from his other side.

Aiden sighed. So his thoughts were plain to see on his face.

"Not really," he admitted. "I want a day where I can just think about what's happening and I don't have to worry about..."

He gestured around, not sure how to put things into words. There was just so much happening! And even in these moments, like right now, when their hands were still, he felt as though his mind was busier than ever.

Eira hummed. "I have an idea. Let's do some math."

Aiden gave her a startled look.

"Let's do some math," she repeated, grinning.

She started firing off questions rapidly, starting with simple problems but slowly making them more and more complex. Aiden's brow pinched with concentration as he fought to keep up with her. After a few minutes, though, he found his tense muscles relaxing and a grin crossing his face.

"Feel better?" Eira asked when they were done.

Aiden nodded. "How do you know to do that?"

Eira shrugged, looking pleased. "I didn't know, but I thought, since math is something you enjoy it might be something that lets your brain rest."

"Thanks." Despite solving such hard problems, his mind felt

much clearer now, as though he'd had a deep sleep that he was now being allowed to wake up from.

Shuang dropped onto the flannel blanket next to Eira. Her hair was plastered against her head and her clothes soaked through.

Aiden glanced out to the misting rain. Shuang must have been standing in it for a long time to get that wet.

"Cold!" Eira cried, shying away from Shuang.

"Sorry." Shuang shifted a few inches away. She glared out of their shelter at Naiser, who was still talking about what the new council's duties would be. "I don't see how adding more people into the government will help when it's the government that's causing all these problems in the first place."

Eira pulled her jacket tighter around herself. "Because we need to have a government that exists to serve everyone, and that can't happen when our voices aren't in their halls."

Shuang groaned as she wrung out her shirt, careful to make it drip off the edges of the blanket. "But don't you see? I'm saying that isn't going to work. The system isn't broken, it just plain doesn't work! We need something different. Something... I don't know. Major. This new council will just end up with their ears blocked like the Elders."

"Why do you think that?" Ryn asked, leaning to get a better look at Shuang around Aiden.

Shuang wrapped her arms around her knees and didn't answer. Because she didn't have anything to say, or because she was afraid of what she had to say?

"Eira, let's trade places," Aiden suggested. "You'll be warmer between Ryn and me."

They shifted around and Aiden settled next to Shuang. He noted she was shivering, too, so he shrugged out of his jacket and offered it to her.

"You'll get cold," Shuang mumbled.

Aiden laughed. "You're the one that has chattering teeth. Come on. We're here for another hour yet; you'll get sick if you don't warm up."

Shuang took the jacket and pulled it over her shoulders.

"I know that this doesn't seem like a perfect solution," Aiden said as he nodded toward Naiser. "Putting in more government when it seems like the current system already doesn't work seems counter-intuitive. So what else could we do? It doesn't seem fair to pull down the system with nothing to replace it."

"That's true," Shuang agreed slowly. She wasn't shivering so much, now.

Naiser finished his speech and stepped down. Aiden was glad to see the recording drones around him. The whole thing would be available to watch on their palmhelds soon. He'd been so busy with Aiden that he missed most of it.

As he sat there with his friends, a thought occurred to him. Why were the Elders doing what they were doing? He'd been frustrated by their actions, had grown increasingly impatient with them, but had never thought to ask why. Not to really ask, at least.

What were the reasons behind the way they were responding to all of this?

"You know what?" he said, leaning his elbows on his knees. "I think we need to learn more about the history of New Vancouver. And before, when they were still the fallout shelter."

"We've already read up on everything, though," Shuang protested.

Eira nodded. "What more could we learn?"

"I'm not sure... but there might be a reason the Elders behave like this. Some cultural thing we're overlooking, maybe," he said, tapping his chin.

"They're acting like this because they're a bunch of—" Shuang stopped herself, biting her tongue.

Ryn leaned back around Eira, laughing. "A bunch of what, Shuang?"

Shuang shook her head, looking rueful. "Sorry. I'm letting my temper get the best of me... again. I just learned that my home bunker has learned that the entire city is riddled with structural cracks.

They're working to fix it, but a single quake could cause everything to collapse. Hundreds of people could die."

Aiden's breath caught in his lungs.

"Are they coming to the surface?" Eira demanded.

Shuang buried her face into her arms. "I don't know. And if they do, will they be allowed to stay here? Or will they be denied? Will they have to split themselves up between other bunkers, or...?"

Eira twisted her hands. "I can't see why New Vancouver wouldn't offer them a place to be, at least."

"Unless they figure it's just a lie to 'steal resources' from them," Shuang mumbled.

Would they, though? Aiden understood things were tense right now, but he thought Shuang was jumping to the worst possible conclusion. Maybe she was right... but he very much hoped that she wasn't.

New Vancouver seemed to be a place where most people at least tried to do the best they could do. The biggest issues were that people disagreed about what 'the best' actually ended up being.

If New Vancouver didn't accept a whole Subterran city of refugees, where would they go? It would put a strain on housing and food, but that would only be temporary. Aiden had read somewhere that there were stores of preserved foods in case they had a shortage. They might run lean on fresh foods but shouldn't they have enough for everyone, especially if the refugees could harvest their underground fields and bring the food with them to the surface?

"I'm afraid that even if they could stay without a problem, they won't be able to adapt to life here," Shuang continued, resting her cheek on her arm now.

The black circles under her eyes spoke to more nights of sleepless night than Aiden had been suffering.

"Then it's a good thing that their options aren't just to stay where they are or come here," Aiden told her gently. "There are other shelters they can seek help from. And if there is a quake coming, we'll be warned plenty in advance with all the equipment dedicated to keeping us safe."

Shuang gave him a weak smile, but seemed unconvinced. Aiden put an arm around her, wishing he could say more. But there were some worries that no words could soothe.

Only action could fix this.

THE NEXT DAY, Naiser, Dawson and Sevilen came to the café to talk to Ryn, Aiden, and Eira. Their expressions were all serious, and they sat together at a table, ordering various drinks and small snacks until the rush died down, then asked to speak with the three.

Aiden glanced at Mama Bunting, who nodded at them. "I'll mark you down as taking a break."

"Thank you," he said.

He took a seat across from Sevilen, with Ryn next to him and Eira at the other end. Ryn folded their hands over the table, expression smooth and calm. Eira worried at her bottom lip with her teeth.

"We have come to ask you three to publicly throw your support to the people who are up for election onto the new council," Sevilen said without preamble, leaning forward. "You're very well-known now, since you not only found the information about the terraforming caches, but also risked your safety to prove they are operable."

Eira's brow furrowed. "So you think people will listen to us, then?"

"Yes," Naiser said.

Aiden sighed heavily. "I'm afraid I can't do this. I won't speak for Ryn and Eira, of course... but I can't in good conscious sway public opinion in this matter. Especially as I filled out the application to run for office myself."

"You... what?" Dawson asked.

"I entered," Aiden replied. "This morning. I looked at the candidates and they're all wonderfully qualified. But I feel as though the best I can do is to be part of this myself, to be a direct part of our policies and change."

Ryn cleared their throat. "I plan to enter as well. It's not something I take lightly, but I think... I think I need to."

"Me, too," Eira confirmed.

"But you're all so young," Dawson protested.

Aiden glanced at his friends. They had talked about this a little bit, but not much. Each one of them had followed this path on their own.

"That's the point," Ryn said.

Dawson's brows puckered together as they stared at Rn, confused.

Ryn smiled, leaning on their elbows. "This new council embodies the voices of those who have been unheard, right? We might be teens, but we have things to say as well. It's a very different for people who have established their lives in one way or another to view things, vs the view that we can bring, when we have all our lives ahead of us.

"Exactly," Eira agreed. "The new council will make policies that might change the trajectory of our entire futures. Shouldn't we have a say?"

Naiser hummed. "If you're old enough to give support to certain candidates, then you're old enough to run yourselves."

"We are," Aiden said firmly.

The three leaders glanced at each other. It appeared that was all they came to ask, because they took their leave then. Once they were gone, Eira let out a shaky breath and shook her head.

"I hadn't decided until just now," she said. "I hope we're making the right choice with this."

Mama Bunting came over, bringing with her three sandwiches. Aiden took his eagerly and devoured it. With how busy he'd been this morning, he had forgotten to eat until now.

"What do you think?" Ryn asked Mama Bunting before she could turn away.

"Oh. Well..." Mama Bunting sighed. "I think you are having far too much responsibility put on you, by others as well as yourselves. But I'm also a Helian and so I don't have the same view on what is happening here as perhaps I ought to."

Aiden wasn't sure exactly what she meant. Did she support their position or not?

"You're going to have a lot of work ahead of you, campaigning and all that. Will you be working to be elected together, or will you each be running your own platform?" Mama Bunting asked.

Aiden rubbed his neck. "I haven't thought about that."

"I'm going to run with the promise that I'll work as hard as I can to get the terraforming equipment up and running," Ryn said.

Eira rested her chin on her hand. "I haven't fully decided mine yet. I think we need to open up the old city more, get resources from there. The tricky part is going to do it respectfully. I know some people will be unhappy no matter what."

"If we can pair the scavenging with something beneficial, like maybe searching for some sort of ancestry records, maybe people will be more open to it," Ryn suggested.

"Maybe. I think, though, it'll have to be something that Helians vote on. They're the ones that have the closest connection to Old Vancouver. So it has to be something that most of them vote on doing."

"That is very kind," Mama Bunting murmured.

Eira shook her head. "Not kind. It's basic decency."

Aiden smiled at her. Even then, he was certain some Helians would consider it grave robbing, but in the end, it would be up to the people to vote on.

"And what about you?" Mama Bunting asked, nodding toward him.

"Education and research. The first thing I'd do is to allow everyone, even non-citizens, to sit the teacher's exams. Everyone who passes will be qualified to teach, and I'll expand on the schooling program to open it up for residents. Then, I'll put more incentives in place for environment and technological research, so we can get the terraforming equipment updated and ensure we know the long-term effects of its usage."

Mama Bunting smiled at them all. Aiden was shocked to see tears glistening in her eyes.

"Are you alright?" he asked her.

"Oh, yes." She wiped her eyes, laughing a little. "Don't mind me. I'm just so proud of the three of you. You don't have to do this, and yet you are."

Aiden smiled back at her, but he knew in his heart she was wrong. They did have to do this. There was too much at stake for them not to be involved in the city of New Vancouver.

The real question was, if their friends and family could see what they were doing, would they have support? Eira talked little about her family and Ryn was an orphan, but all three had friends. Aiden tried to visualize Pat and what she might say. He knew what Richmond and Laura would say—but then, they'd find a reason to be nasty to him, no matter what.

With a jolt, he realized that in the last three months since he'd been above ground, he'd made a choice. He didn't know when he made it, but he'd made it all the same.

He would never go back below the surface. The above-ground was his home.

RYN ROLLED their neck as they tried to work out a kink in their shoulder. An exhausting election campaign had run for a full week now. They thought it ought to have been longer, to allow more people to enter, but there would be a review and re-election in one year's time. They imagined a lot more people would run to be elected at that point.

"Are you ready?" Eira asked them.

"I guess so," Ryn answered.

Their stomach swooped as they heard the noise from the crowd outside of the little room where the candidates all were. Ryn, Aiden, and Eira were the three youngest candidates... and they were going to learn the results of the election soon. It was being double-checked right now to make sure the first tally was correct.

Ryn didn't like the waiting on something so important. Oh, they didn't want it rushed. They just wished that time wasn't moving quite so slowly. They swung their arms, trying to release the excess energy pent up in them.

"Calm down," Aiden told them.

"Easier said than done," Ryn grumbled back.

Aiden gave them a wry smile. "Yeah, sorry. I know that's not helpful. Here."

He offered Ryn a hand, and Ryn took it. Then Eira joined them, forming a little circle. The three looked at each other, feeling the bond that had developed over these last few months since they arrived in New Vancouver.

"Whatever happens, I'm proud of all of us," Eira said. She gave Ryn's hand a squeeze. "We have done what we could make this world a better place. Even if we aren't elected, we're going to keep pushing for things to get better."

Aiden nodded. "It's been tiring, but we can't give up. So long as we're working together, we really can make a great change here. Look at how much we've helped already."

Ryn gave them both a small smile. They were right, of course. The Elders had finally released an official statement. Basically, they would accept the voices of the people for this New Council and once elected, the two councils could get together to discuss what was to be done. Still nothing on the terraforming equipment, but this was better than nothing.

"We're going to do this," Ryn murmured softly. They straightened, chin jutting forward as their eyes grew more determined. "No matter what happens, we will create a world where everyone is welcome, no matter what. Whether it's New Vancouver or if we have to create our own city."

Eira laughed softly and hugged them. "I'm so glad you're both with me."

"Me, too," Ryn said fervently.

"Same," Aiden agreed. "I couldn't have come this far without you."

A voice rang out through the room, interrupting them. "The election results are in."

Heart pounding, Ryn turned to the screen where the names of the New Council were up. There, at the bottom of the list... Ryn, Eira, Aiden.

Triumph, relief, and an unfamiliar weight settled on Ryn all at once. So this was it... The dawning of a new day. They would take this responsibility to heart. There was so much to be done.

16

HEAR MY VOICE

EIRA BRAIDED her jet-black hair into a tight braid, then pinned it up at the nape. It wasn't the most attractive hairstyle, at least among Aerians. But it would keep her hair out of her way as well as protect it from potential damage. She anticipated an endless day today, and she'd rather not risk ruining what she considered her best feature.

The promised meeting between Elders and the new council had not yet happened, but it would soon. She was certain of it. For the time being, she had to look over a few drafts for proposals that the other members of the new Council wanted to present to the people.

As she stepped out of the shared bathroom at the hostel, she found Aiden and Ryn both looking at their palmhelds, frowning.

"What is it?" she asked.

"We both got notices from the residency board. You should check yours," Aiden said.

Eira pulled out her palmheld, surprised to see that she had a notification she'd missed. She skimmed through the message and her jaw dropped.

"They're threatening to take away my residency!" she exclaimed.

Ryn shoved their palmheld into their pocket. "Yeah. Ours, too. Apparently, we're not logging enough hours at our place of work."

Eira scrolled through the message again before she turned the palmheld off. Her chest felt tight and her teeth ground together. What was the meaning of this? Was it the Elders trying to exert power over the new council or was it a clerical error?

"We've been so busy with the election, I didn't even notice we were falling behind on our hours," Aiden murmured. He kept studying the message. "The way this is worded... I'm not sure that working with the New Council is going to count toward a permanent job."

"How could it not?" Ryn demanded, outraged.

Aiden sighed as he finally put his palmheld away as well. "Because we're not being paid for it. I don't know. We'll have to see if anyone else got these messages."

"And bring up the possibility of it being a job," Ryn groaned.

Eira pressed her fingertips to her temples, trying to work through her emotions. She was surprised at how betrayed this made her feel. The three of them had fought so hard to be included on the new council and they had been elected by vote. If the Elders withdrew their residency, what would it mean?

They wouldn't be allowed to stay at the hostel, for one thing. They wouldn't have money to spend on their necessities. People weren't driven out of the city but if they couldn't meet their basic needs, what choice would they have?

Eira pictured herself living beneath a blanket in some alley, picking food off the wall-gardens to survive, huddling with Aiden and Ryn to keep warm on frosty nights.

Maybe Shuang would give them a place to live.

"Come on." Aiden grasped her elbow and pulled her to her feet. "We will not get anything done sitting around here. We've got a council meeting."

Eira nodded, grounding herself again. The three of them headed out—Yaella and Ayasha wished them luck—and made their commute toward the temporary New Council chambers. They'd been given a room on the ground floor of the Elder's building in city center. It was cramped with the table and chairs brought into it, but it was passable for now.

The meeting started with Naiser delivering some solemn news. "The Elders have postponed our meeting with them. Elder Francis suffered a stroke last night and is in the hospital. They are waiting to see if he'll be able to continue to serve or needs to be replaced."

Eira's stomach twisted. Elder Francis was the one that seemed to have actually listened to her and the others when they were with the Elders. She hoped he'd be alright.

"We have also received a letter," Naiser continued. "I'll send it to all your palmhelds so you can read it again later. It starts with, 'To the council'."

Eira leaned forward, eager to hear what the letter had to say. But as Naiser read it, her eyes grew wider and wider. The whole letter was chastising them for not moving fast enough. They demanded that the terraforming equipment be dug up and activated immediately, and it appeared most of the letter was telling the new council that they were useless because they hadn't sent out teams yet.

One particular line stood out to Eira, "With all the Subterrans in the city, there should be plenty of muscle to get this started immediately."

She glanced over at Ryn to find them just as flabbergasted, but Aiden sat with his head back and eyes closed. He seemed to absorb each word. Once Naiser was done reading the letter, a silence settled over the council. Nobody seemed to know how to respond.

Finally, Ryn spoke up. "We haven't had the time to get started on any of that, though! I'm still looking for qualified engineers to study the equipment we found on Vancouver Island."

"Are we sure that was written in good faith?" Eira asked doubtfully. "It sounded like they assumed that the Subterrans would all be sent to dig up the equipment based on them being more suited to physical labor. Which is something that a lot of Helians seem to think."

Naiser shook his head. "Let's not start making assumptions about the character of the letter-writer. We must approach it as a legitimate concern. Ryn, we will need you to write up a report on the processes you plan to use to put together these teams."

Ryn nodded, sighing.

"That isn't the only letter we've received, though," another of the council members said. "I received one yesterday condemning the use of terraforming, stating that it's a destructive process and will create more problems than it will resolve. It called for us to do something about the wolf rats."

Eira replaced a groan. But this was why they had so many council members, right? Someone else could take on the Wolf Rats while Aiden and she helped Ryn with the terraforming project.

She straightened. "I'll start a polling process to get a more thorough understanding about how the city feels about terraforming. But I can't imagine that Ryn, Aiden and I would have been elected if the majority of the people weren't in favor of it."

"Still, a poll is wise," Naiser told her, nodding his approval.

The meeting turned to other things. Namely, one of the underground bunkers was demanding trade renegotiations and with the Elders out of commission because of Francis' stroke, that left the new council to deal with it.

It was long. By the time the meeting was over, Eira wasn't sure exactly what all had been decided. She would have to go through the notes when she got back home. It was dark out. She and her friends were silent as they headed back home.

"I wish we had homes closer to the city center," she sighed once they got back to the hostel. Food was waiting for them, but she was so tired she didn't have the energy to eat.

As she crawled into bed, though, it occurred to her—they hadn't talked about the letter that the three of them had received about their residency.

Maybe tomorrow, she told herself, closing her eyes. Or maybe this is something we'll have to deal with ourselves.

EIRA BIT back a yawn as she brought a coffee to a customer. Ryn had gone to the residency board today to get answers about the notifications that the three of them received while Aiden was meeting with Naiser to see if some sort of payment system could be implemented.

In the last week since being elected, the three of them had put in more hours with the council than they ever had with Mama Bunting's café. Today, Eira was trying to pull up her weekly amount of residency work hours. If she didn't, she'd end up having to take on a second job to get the hours she needed for the month.

"You're one of those kids on the New Council, aren't you?" the aquatic sitting at the table demanded.

"Yes. Miss Eira," she said.

The aquatic scowled. "Miss Vonn. What are you doing here, at a café?"

Eira blinked at Vonn, scrambling to understand why Vonn had such an acidic tone. "Well, you see I am still on residency and so I need a certain number of hours—"

"Why aren't you dealing with the sewer leakage over on the east side?" Vonn interrupted. "We've had a backup for three days now and there's been nothing done to fix the issue! If you're part of the council, you should be working on that rather than wasting your time with coffee."

Tension crept up Eira's neck, pulling a strain at the back of her head. "I'm aware of the situation. Councilor Ben was assigned to take care of the problem. He's currently cleaning out the system with cleaner robots so that they can repair the leaks."

"The smell is driving me crazy. You should be doing something," Vonn said.

"I know that it's frustrating. I assure you, Councilor Ben is hard at work on this. The pipes are old and have broken through in several places." Eira smiled sympathetically at the Aquatic. "Ben says he thinks it'll be taken care of tomorrow."

"It should have been taken care of yesterday! And you're sitting here serving coffee."

Eira sighed. Why was she getting the feeling that Vonn only wanted someone to complain to? Well, she wasn't going to put up with it. She turned and walked away, to the next table, who was waiting for her.

Vonn stood. "Hey! I'm talking to you."

"Excuse me," Mama Bunting said, stepping between Eira and Vonn. "There will be none of that in my café. Eira gave you the answers you needed. If you're just here to harass her, get out."

Vonn sank back down, grumbling. But she didn't bother Eira for the rest of her shift—a testament to just how powerful a presence Mama Bunting actually had.

Eira sent a silent prayer of thanks to her ancestors for putting her in Mama Bunting's path, along with Ryn and Aiden. They couldn't have gotten this far without her support.

"AND THAT IS why we need engineers for the project," Eira said.

She stood at a podium in a theater classroom. Every seat was taken by students who were all four or more years older than she was. She'd elected to wear her flowy, light robes from Fata Morgana, leaning into her Aerian roots. Helians seemed to respond better when she wore them.

"We have signup sheets to volunteer for the teams heading to Vancouver Island. If this is something you're interested in, please leave your name and how to contact you," Eira concluded. She had spent the last hour describing what their plans were.

Ryn had got a lead engineer for the project, but they needed many more trained individuals if it was going to be successful.

Eira stepped back from the podium when something sailed through the air. It smacked her right in the chest, causing her to jump back with a cry of shock and alarm. A wet, sticky piece of watermelon pulp dropped from her front to the floor. She stared at it with a slack jaw as raucous laughter started in the audience. Most of the students were muttering to each other disapprovingly, but there were a handful of students right at the front who started jeering.

"That is enough!" Professor Bellows erupted, drawing Eira back from the podium. His eyes flashed as he glared at the group of unruly students.

The theater fell silent.

One of the laughing students got to their feet. "You're right, Professor. It is enough. We don't need to listen to this usurper anymore."

Usurper? Eira gaped. In what world was she an usurper?

Another of the students jumped up. "That's right! The Elders have every right to drive them from our city! We don't have enough food to feed everyone in the world, and yet she and the others like her think we should just absorb all citizenship from other places? What do we get back from it?"

Professor Bellows opened his mouth, but Eira put up a hand. Though her heart pounded with adrenaline, she couldn't let him answer this for her.

"I understand that food scarcity is a genuine fear among the Helians. The brave founders of New Vancouver suffered so much and went through their own periods of starvation. It's only natural that you're still afraid of that being repeated."

Eira paused to check the response. The two students who were standing looked angry, as though they were hoping she'd say something that they could have attacked. She smoothed her shaking hands over her front.

"This is where the wisdom of the Elder council comes into play," she continued. "They have been taking action to counter possible shortages for years now. There are huge stockpiles of dehydrated, freeze-dried, and otherwise preserved foods, as well as the hardy plants that produce year-round in our climate."

A few of the students in the crowd nodded.

"The purpose of this terraforming project isn't to simply bring everyone in the world to this city," Eira continued. "It's pulling the residual toxins from the environment, opening up more space for humanity to return to the surface of the planet. There are food shortages in other settlements; we want to give them the means of increasing their own production."

"And why should our labor go to serve them when they've given us nothing in return?" the angry student demanded.

Eira didn't know how to answer that. To her, it was simple. Give them the means to produce their own food and everyone's lives will be better. There might be a time in the future when they needed that aid.

But even not, if New Vancouver could help others, especially at low-cost to itself, why would it be such a hardship to share that help?

Before she could answer, a student from the back of the classroom yelled, "It's helping us, too, you dingbat! You're just mad that you failed your last exam."

Eira's shoulders slumped as the classroom erupted. Were they going to get any help at all? This project was important, and yet it seemed like people were more interested in arguing about things that didn't matter...

As Professor Bellows struggled to get everyone calmed down, Eira couldn't help but wonder if this was what the Elders went through, too. And if maybe they deserved a bit more grace.

LATE THAT NIGHT, Eira lay in her little cubbyhole bed, staring blankly into the darkness. Her body was so heavy she didn't have the strength to get out of bed. Her mind raced, whirling from one thought to the next. It wouldn't allow her to sleep, no matter how much she wanted to.

What were her parents up to right now? What about her sisters? An ache settled in her chest, making tears spring to her eyes. She missed them so badly! What wouldn't she do to have a conversation with them? They'd all be shocked to see what she'd done with herself here in New Vancouver.

She was shocked, too. All of her life she had been confined to a single building, and she'd never thought she would do anything active with her existence. Now here she was, in a council of her own.

Maybe those students at the speech were right. Maybe she didn't have enough real-world experiences to be worthy of this position.

She groaned as she rolled over and shimmied out of bed. There was no point in laying here and beating herself up for the choices she'd made so far. She padded out of the bedroom toward the kitchen, where she was surprised to find Ryn there, making themself some food.

"Hey," Eira greeted. "Want any help?"

"Sure. Can you get the almond milk out?"

Eira opened the fridge. "Is cow's milk okay?"

"No, I need the almond taste."

Eira sorted through the available milks and grabbed the one labeled 'almond.'

Ryn thanked her and added some milk. "This is a recipe that my friend Aalton used to help him sleep. I'm hoping it will work for me, too. I just have so many thoughts in my head."

"Me, too," Eira agreed. "I just keep thinking about how everything is way more complicated than I thought it was. How there's always someone who wants one thing, then someone who wants the opposite. I can't help but feel like we judged the Elders too harshly."

"Maybe," Ryn said slowly.

Eira took a seat at the table, resting her head in her hand.

"I think we were right to be frustrated, though," Ryn continued. They stirred the mixture they had on the stove, focused on their work. "Even if the Elders couldn't decide on a course of action or if they had to balance all the different wants and needs, I still think it was poor form for them to just be so silent."

"You're probably right."

Ryn nodded once. "I'm going to go to the Elder Council tomorrow. I don't care about not having a meeting scheduled. We need to have some sort of understanding about their perspective... otherwise, all of this is going to fall apart."

Eira shivered. Ryn was right, of course. "I'll go, too."

"And I will," Aiden said from the doorway.

Eira smiled at him as he came into the kitchen. The three sat in silence, and Eira's stomach tightened further. Would this be what they needed to finally break through? Would they be able to build a united New Vancouver...

Or were they all too divided already?

RYN TWISTED THEIR HANDS, nerves fluttering in their chest as they, Eira, and Aiden marched up the stairs to the where the Elder Council took their meetings. It felt bold and daring to do this, even though they were being escorted.

Maybe it was because the official meeting between the New Council and the Elders was still a ways away yet. But if they were going to have any forward momentum, then they all needed to understand each other. Ryn was just glad that when they had asked permission to meet with the Elders, the Elders had agreed, despite Elder Francis still being in the hospital.

The three of them were escorted into the Council Room. Unlike the few other times where they'd been here, this time the room held a table, around which all the Elders sat. Three empty chairs sat near the head of the table.

"Please, take a seat," Elder Suzanne said to them. Dark bruises were under her eyes.

Ryn sat, focused on Suzanne. "Are you alright? Did you fall?"

Suzanne gave them a shocked look. "Why would you ask that?"

"Your face is so covered in bruises," Ryn answered.

Suzanne laughed softly as she shook her head. "No, no, child. This is because of my sleepless nights."

"Oh."

"Before we begin," Suzanne said slowly, "I want to offer my apologies to you three. I've acted poorly toward you. I should have been trying to bridge the gap between our generations, and instead, I've been rude and dismissive."

Ryn gave her a tentative smile. "Thank you. We really appreciate hearing that. That's why we're here. To bridge the gap. You have all kept this city safe and prosperous for years. What we don't understand is why you won't answer our questions."

The Elders glanced at each other. It seemed, though, that they had decided that Suzanne would speak for them today, as they all ended up looking at her.

Suzanne folded her hands on the table, staring at her fingertips, as though deep in thought. "We thought you might ask this. So let me share with you a little about how this council is meant to work."

Elder Megan lifted a hand. "Before we begin that, let's all get some water here, shall we? We don't want our New Council members to end up parched."

She gave the three a kindly smile. Ryn nodded their thanks. Maybe it was part of being an Aquatic, but over the last few months, they'd realized that they drank a lot more water than either Eira or Aiden. It would be fascinating to delve deeper into that, to know what adaptations actually stuck... but when would they have the time for that?

Water was brought and glasses given to everyone. It took longer than Ryn wanted. They found their toes tapping impatiently and forced themself to stop.

I promised myself I'd be patient.

Once things were settled again, Elder Suzanne spoke.

"In the beginning of New Vancouver, we nearly failed before we'd built the city," she explained. "Everyone had a different idea about what we should do. It led to a great deal of strife. One camp made a move and blocked another camp from getting their goals. It was unorganized and chaotic.

"It was this time that the council—not Elders, because there were no Elders surviving in that generation," Suzanne continued, "—The council decided they would stop all these divisions. That it would only speak once the Elders could decide on the same thing to say. And it served us well, at that time."

Aiden hummed. "So that's why you've been silent for so long, despite everything we've done? Because there were divisions among your council and you couldn't agree on the same thing to say?"

Suzanne nodded.

"I'm sorry, but I don't think that's good enough," Eira said. Her brows were pinched and she shifted uncomfortably, showing just how difficult it was for her to speak up like this. "Even if you couldn't agree on a course of action, you should have told us you heard us. That's what we were asking for. To be heard."

A few Elders looked triumphant at this, though they quickly rearranged their expression to be less smug.

Ryn hid their own smile. It appeared as though these Elders weren't all that different from the ones that they knew after all.

"Perhaps you are right," Suzanne said, frowning. "But this is how we have always done things. For all the years I've been on the Elder Council, I have never seen such a division among our ranks. It's been... worrying. More than one of us feared this would spell the end of New Vancouver."

Eira leaned back in her chair. She glanced at Ryn and gave a tiny nod.

Ryn's butterflies returned. They'd had a different relationship with the Elders under the Dome than Aiden had had in Bunk 37 or Eira had in Fata Morgana. Therefore, the three of them had decided that Ryn should be the one doing the talking.

"I understand that we have been calling for a great deal of change over these last few weeks," Ryn said, clasping their hands around their glass of water. "And we three understand that perhaps it is too dramatic a change too quickly. We're young and impatient. So we're not here today to demand change."

"Aren't you?" Suzanne asked.

Megan stroked her chin, looking intrigued.

"No. We're not here as an official representation of the New Council when I asked permission to meet," Ryn answered. Their hands tightened on the glass. "We want answers. Not as one voice, not even as anything that is one truth. We just want to hear your voices, just as we want you to hear ours."

They drank a big gulp of water. Somehow, this seemed to be even more nerve-wracking than if they had come in here and demanded that all the Elders resign their positions at once. Maybe because reaching out with questions and hoping for a vulnerable answer was something vulnerable in and of itself.

"I don't understand," Suzanne said. Her face was twisted in concentration. "You want to hear... what? What questions do you have that we can answer?"

Ryn turned to Eira, gesturing at her. Eira was the one that had done most of the reading about New Vancouver's history, after all. Eira's normally blue-tinged skin was paler than usual and her eyes were slightly wide.

When Ryn glanced at Aiden, they saw he looked just as nervous. His normal steady gaze kept flitting between all the Elders, like he wasn't sure where to look. It somehow made Ryn feel a bit better to know that their friends were just as nervous as they were.

"There aren't many first-hand accounts of what happened when New Vancouver was still being built," Eira said. "But it was your parents and grandparents that lived through the cloud. It was their parents that lived in the before days, and they're the ones that spent their childhood in the days before the cloud. So they're the ones that witnessed the destruction first-hand."

Megan sighed as she nodded. "Our parents and grandparents did live through that. We have recorded what stories they'd share, but you can understand why we had much more pressing things to deal with, rather than getting those words."

"But you see, that's the problem," Eira said as she leaned forward. "There aren't enough words. For too long the Elders have remained silent, not wanting to expression anything without a united front. But the thing is, your silence has caused harm. We don't know enough about the before days."

Aiden cleared his throat. "There's a saying in Bunk 37. The past has forged a path for us. Those who refuse to use that path are those who will be mired in the same pitfalls our ancestors fought to overcome."

"We have a saying here," Megan said with a wry smile. "Those who don't know history are doomed to repeat it."

"And that's the very thing we're needing to know," Ryn said. "History. What brought New Vancouver to where it is today, so we can understand what pitfalls to avoid as we move forward. There's no unity in New Vancouver."

Eira nodded her agreement. "There is, however, another problem... the idea that unity can only be achieved when everyone says the same thing. But that's not true. Think about the harmony of music. It's not all the same note. The beauty comes from the differences. And that is exactly what New Vancouver needs. To be united in a harmony, not same-mindedness."

Suzanne frowned at her. "To continue your metaphor, everyone in the music has to be singing the same song, though. Otherwise, it's just so much noise."

Ah, that was true. Eira hadn't considered that. Her brain scrambled to come up with a response, but it was Ryn that answered.

"The metaphor might be perfect, but we're not here to squabble about that. We're talking about everyone agreeing on the same course of action versus the same forward momentum. We can take different paths to reach the same destination."

Aiden cleared his throat. "The only way all the voices in the city can say the same thing is if some of them set aside their wants and wishes in favor of the wants and wishes of the whole. You want a place that's safe and comfortable for everyone and that so commendable."

"But?" Suzanne asked with a wry smile.

"But your approach is that everyone's safety and comfort looks the same as yours did in your youth. Look at the residency require- ments," Aiden continued. "We need to have so many work hours. We need to have a permanent place to live. They fill the need to give purpose and daily needs. But it gives no room to plan for the future."

Eira nodded. "I'm afraid that there are several policies that think only of the immediate needs."

Ryn leaned forward. "My colleagues are quite right. So that leads me to believe that you have immediate concerns for why you are opposed to using the terraforming equipment."

Right. Eira took a deep breath and released it. It was so easy to get off track in this! It was just more proof that these things were more difficult than she'd anticipated. Even now, the Elders were glancing at each other with serious expressions that made Eira think that there was something else going to be brought up at any moment.

"I am not sure that this is something we will share with you," Suzanne said.

Ryn opened their mouth, only to close it when Aiden put a hand on their shoulder. Their eyes flashed and the tension coiling through them was obvious.

"Why?" Eira asked, fighting to keep her voice level. Even now, the Elders were going to give them the silent treatment?

Her heart sank. Was there any point to any of this anymore?

AIDEN'S BROW furrowed as he studied the Elders. They all seemed extremely tired. He could imagine the sleepless nights they'd been suffering with the weight of the city on them. How many letters had they been receiving? How much criticism that felt as though it wasn't helpful to anyone?

I have a different story than Ryn and Eira. Ryn came to the surface because their home had failed. Eira came because her life would have been cut short. I came to stay only a year and then return.

Of course, that had changed, but the point remained the same. Eira and Ryn came to the surface with no way of returning home. The same wasn't true of him. He could just wait and then return to Bunk 37, to his family and friends.

"Can we even talk about this, if you won't tell us why you're opposed to the terraforming?" Eira asked, sounding utterly defeated.

"You are all very young. You don't know the weight of responsibility that comes with taking care of others," Suzanne said.

Aiden straightened. He wasn't going to give up like this! "No. We don't. But, if I might ask, how many of you were born underground?"

Suzanne frowned.

Elder Megan leaned forward. "We all were, except my daughter, Sylvia," she nodded to the woman next to her. "My mother, Elder Lindsey, was the one who first left the below to find the sun again. I was a child at the time, only five years old. I only knew life below the surface and begged my mother to take me home. But she knew better than I did."

There was a delicate weight on her words, as though reminding the three that they were, by all accounts, still transitioning out of their childhoods. Of course they couldn't understand everything... what was frustrating to Aiden was the increasing feeling that, even though they had come to hear from the Elders, they weren't being told anything.

Except they did.

He stood and bowed toward the Elders. "Please, may I have a moment to speak with Ryn and Eira?"

"Of course," Megan replied.

His friends looked confused, but Aiden gestured for them to step into the hall with him. He closed the door lightly and turned to them. It was as though a lightbulb had lit inside his head.

"We're approaching this the wrong way," he murmured. "We've made a big mistake in all of this."

Ryn frowned at him. "What do you mean?"

"I mean, they said that they need to discuss and have a unified voice. We then explained how we feel like unity doesn't mean the same, but they haven't been able to discuss it!" He looked between them, gauging their reactions.

Ryn's eyes widened with understanding and Eira made a little 'O' with her mouth.

"We want them to listen to us, so we have to listen to them. And they're saying they can't give us answered without being able to discuss it among themselves first," he said. "So we need to back off. We need to listen."

Eira nodded slowly, then fixed her eyes on him. "Tell them your story. The full story. You were born underground, like them. Your parents made the same hard choice as theirs, to risk the surface in the hope of a better life. I can't really relate. My journey was from Fata Morgana to another Aerian settlement."

"And I had that painting," Ryn murmured. "I had something that gave me hope, a mystery to uncover. Something from the past to push me to the future. But you didn't have that. You had no real assurances."

Aiden considered this for a moment, then nodded. "Alright. Then let's go back in. We'll tell our stories. All of us. Because we each bring a new perspective to this."

He held his hands out to his friends, and they shook. Then, the three of them gave each other encouraging smiles and stepped through the doors. It was time to share their stories.

IT WAS A FURTHER three days before the New council met with the Elder Council. Ryn put on their best clothes for the meeting, knowing this would be far different from the last time they talked with the Elders. They had a better perspective now, though, and would be ready to step back and look at things from a new lens if need be.

Elder Megan started the meeting. "Thank you all for being here. I know that we have tested your patience for some time now, and we are grateful that you are still willing to have a dialogue with us."

Naiser, who had been chosen to speak for the New Council, nodded at her. "We are pleased that we will have this dialogue. How is Elder Francis?"

"Released from the hospital," Megan answered, and Ryn sighed in relief. "However, he will not be rejoining the council. The announcement will be given this afternoon, along with the time for a new election to be held to replace him."

Ryn winced. So Francis was that bad, was he? They hoped that he'd be able to recover from his stroke. They surreptitiously made a note in their palmheld to send a well-wishing note to Francis.

"We're all hoping that he is comfortable and will live the rest of his life with peace," Naiser said. He bowed his head a moment, then added, "I understand this may seem macabre to some, seeing as I'm not wishing for health. But this is a traditional blessing in Fata Morgana."

Eira nodded beside Aiden.

"Thank you." Megan rested her hands on the table. "Now. We will speak about the terraforming equipment, but before we do that, we would like to address an issue of residency."

Ryn straightened as Aiden shifted in his seat, looking intrigued.

"We have known there are some people within the city who are unhappy that residents have been allowed to be elected, rather than full citizens," Megan continued.

Ryn's stomach tightened. Was she going to say the Elders had demanded they and their friends stand down?

"However, since the New Council was made in answer to the current system, we will not make any official statement regarding the New Council's internal structure." Megan sighed. "We will, however, release a new statement concerning the role of the Elders. We will keep our policies. We will not condemn or condone any policy or action unless we all agree."

"No," Aiden breathed under his breath. He looked crestfallen.

Megan caught this and smiled at him. "It's a good thing, then, that the New Council is under no such obligations. We will have to discuss the division of authority and responsibilities, of course, but we are proud of all of you for stepping up in this role. And we say with one voice, we're sorry that our silence required it."

"I..." Naiser cleared his throat. "I think I can speak for the New Council when I say thank you. We will discuss the need of residency or citizenship among ourselves."

Megan nodded. "The Elders have a proposition. First, we firmly believe that no government position should pay money. It should, however, be counted as 'work' toward residency and those in the government should be given permanent residence within the city."

Which meant that Ryn, Aiden, and Eira would no longer have to run themselves ragged between working and trying to move things with the New Council. Ryn smiled, pleased.

"The matter of education can be discussed at a later time." Megan looked at her wrinkled hands and stretched them out, sighing. "Which, of course, brings us to the central conflict our city has been facing. The terraforming equipment."

Everyone seemed to lean in closer at this. Ryn's mind whirled—were they finally going to learn why the Elders were so reluctant to use the equipment?

"Ryn, Aiden and Eira asked us recently why we were opposed to using the terraforming equipment. And that is the same answer why we kept it a secret." Megan nodded to her daughter, Syliva. "I will explain while Elder Sylvia brings Elder Lindsey to join us."

Surprise rippled through Ryn's body. After meeting with the

council for so long and never meeting Elder Lindsey, they had started to assume that she was more of a figurehead than anything else. After all, she would have to be over a hundred years old by now...

Sylvia slipped from the room and Megan took a drink from her water, then sighed. "Sadly, the terraforming equipment that was buried in caches across the globe is exactly what caused the devastation in the first place."

Eira gasped, then her pale blue skin turned lilac with a blush.

"I've never heard of anything like that before," Naiser said, his eyes wide.

"Yes, because it was one of the things the Elders agreed to keep a secret. We never thought that the caches would be discovered, so why put that sort of fear in people's hearts?" Megan shook her head. "In the old days, humans were terrible to their planet. They stripped its resources from deep within the crust. They poisoned the atmosphere and melted the ice caps."

"Why?" Aiden burst out, looking stunned.

"Not on purpose. As a side effect of their activities. And so they created the terraforming equipment. Their clever machines flew, walked on the ground, and swam through the deeps, collecting all that pollution. They then drilled deep into the arctic, and poured their excess pollution deep, deep into the earth. If it was there, it would not harm them..."

Megan shook her head, looking old and sad.

Ryn rubbed the back of their neck, imagining the people of the old days, trying to fix the problems they created. "So what happened? What went wrong?"

"The terraforming equipment that worked to restore the ice caps went too deep in the wrong spot. The pollutants froze, and in the freezing cracked the crust of the earth. The people worked to contain the breach, but it was too deep, too wide, and the ice couldn't hold it back." Megan shook her head, sighing. "Suzanne. I can't keep going."

Suzanne reached over to squeeze Morgan's hand, then took up where she left off. "The ice-cap terraforming equipment worked hard to keep it in, but they weren't meant for continual work. They died and then summer came. The frozen pollutants thawed and were released as gases into the air, forming the cloud that killed our world."

Naiser held his face in his hands.

To Ryn's surprise, it was Eira that broke the silence. "And the equipment in the artic started up again, didn't it? But something had gone wrong. It reversed the ice... and sent the cloud even further."

"Yes." Suzanne's voice was little more than a whisper. "We only learned about it after we established contact with Fata Morgana... but it was a team of Aerians that went to that equipment and sacrificed their lives to stop the cycle. New Vancouver had already been established by that time.

"If not for a city we hadn't even known of, this city would have been destroyed in its infancy."

Megan sighed. "So you see? The equipment is dangerous. That's why we kept it a secret. Because if we use it... we'll just be making the same mistakes as our ancestors."

18

WEAVING A UNIFIED FORCE

AIDEN BLEW OUT A HEAVY BREATH, his eyes burning. A heaviness weighed on his shoulders as he considered what the Elders had just shared with them. He leaned forward, his hands clasped over the table as he studied them.

"What do you fear will happen, then?" he asked softly.

Suzanne sighed heavily. She took a drink of water while Megan glanced at her. It was clear Suzanne was exhausted from speaking, though, so Megan took over.

"The equipment will solidify and keep the pollutants they scrub out of the systems. It's why we have stopped cleaning out the environment around New Vancouver. We had to figure out what to do with the pollutants that were cleaned out from this space, and we dumped it into the ocean," Megan answered, her expression sorrowful.

Ryn gasped.

Megan shook her head, expression regretful. "We didn't know about the Aquatics. We stopped the program as soon as we realized some people had moved to below the ocean's surface. But where will it go if we keep scrubbing out the pollutants now? We'll have a buildup, just like the old days, and we risk releasing it again."

Ryn rested their elbows on the table, expression warring between emotions. Aiden reached out and laid a gentle hand on their shoulder, trying to support them.

The Dome failed because of the ocean's acidity. It must be a tremendous shock to realize that New Vancouver was directly responsible for increasing that acidity. Would their home have held longer without the terraforming activities of the city?

"Technology has changed, though," Aiden said, looking back to the Elders. "In Bunk 37, we ran into a similar problem while mining out the lower levels. And so we developed a technology that actually breaks down the individual molecules of the pollutants and reforms them into something else. The same thing can be used here."

"It isn't that simple," Megan protested.

"No, not simple," Eira agreed. "But possible."

Suzanne shook her head. "We need to be sure we aren't causing even more problems before we can even think of using such a means."

Aiden sighed, shaking his head. They didn't get it, did they? "That's just the point. We already know how it works. We already know it doesn't have further issues, because it's been the means used to break down dangerous gasses to something harmless."

"Not in conjunction with terraforming equipment, though," Megan pointed out.

"Because we don't have terraforming equipment," Aiden answered.

Megan nodded. "Exactly. So we don't know if the technology of Bunk 37 will, in fact, work with this equipment."

Frustration welled in Aiden's chest. Why did it feel like they were talking at cross purposes here? He wasn't saying that they should just throw everything together with shoelace and chewing gum. No, he suggested that they combine this technology.

"This is why all the technology here in New Vancouver and in the various other settlements should be open for everyone," Ryn said. They threw back their shoulders. "Because by keeping everything so insular and regulating people from other settlements to menial labor, you have lost out on years' worth of working together."

Eira nodded her agreement. "We should be coming together to figure it out. We should use the technology from Bunk 37 in combination with the terraforming equipment so we can work out the kinks. The answer isn't just to not do anything because it might go wrong."

Aiden straightened, bolstered by his friends' statements. "Yes, exactly. If we can all bring our survival strategies together and share the knowledge, each settlement has discovered, then we can find a way to work together out of this."

Aiden stood and strode to the space in the middle of the room, not taken up by the table. Eira and Ryn followed him, then the three of them stood, with Ryn in their center.

"This has to change," Ryn said, their voice carrying through. "We have to stop this isolation, we have to stop acting as though we have an individual responsibility. We may be Aquatic, Subterran and Aerian, but we are all still human. We have to work together!"

The doors to the chamber opened. Elder Sylvia reentered, pushing a wheelchair with her. In the wheelchair was the wizened form of Elder Lindsey.

Aiden couldn't tear his eyes away. He thought that the other Elders were old, but Lindsey was older than anyone he'd seen before. She was tiny, hunched over in her chair. Her head barely reached the top. Her skin was thin and translucent, hands knobbed with arthritis.

"Greetings," the little woman called, her voice thin. "My grand-daughter tells me there is a matter of urgency for which I must attend this meeting. Which is odd, considering that I haven't been elected to be part of this council since my one-hundredth birthday."

She chuckled to herself, the sound stronger than her voice. Aiden swallowed hard. That was right... she was one-hundred and ten years old, according to the city records.

"Come closer," she said, beckoning to them. "What have you come to tell us?"

Aiden glanced at the others.

Ryn chewed their lip, then threw their shoulders back. "We want the terraforming caches buried by the old ones to be released. We want to combine them with new technology to break down the pollutants, not merely remove them from the land. We want to make this world habitable for everyone who wishes to live on the surface."

"Mmmm." Lindsey shook her head slowly. "I have lived through a great deal, children. I remember the days when my people starved to death. I remember the horrible tragedies when we tried to come to the surface. I remember the days of scarcity."

"That is the past, though," Eira said.

"A past all too fresh in our minds," Suzanne interjected.

Aiden stepped forward and bowed toward Lindsey. "Eldest Lindsey. We have come with a plea. Let go of the past and embrace the future. Otherwise, everything will have been in vain."

Lindsey folded her hands and smiled, a twinkle in her clouded eyes. "Funny how things have come full circle, isn't it? What with you three leading an uprising against the Elder Council?"

Aiden's cheeks turned warm. "Well... I'm not sure I would say it was an uprising."

"You very much did," Lindsey replied. "You resisted the status quo, rebelled against the order of things. Just because it wasn't violent doesn't mean it wasn't an uprising. I'm just remembering how I helped to lead an uprising myself. I wasn't as young as you were."

She fell silent, closing her eyes. Had she fallen asleep, or was she remembering?

"Now we have come to a new uprising. A new generation who can't see the horrors of the past so clearly. A generation who can only see their hopes for the future," she continued, then opened her eyes again. "What are your plans once the caches are released?"

Aiden floundered for a moment. He wasn't sure if this was some sort of trick question, lingering a little too long on what else Lindsey had said. Were they blinding themselves to the past? But wasn't that exactly the reason they were here, so that it didn't become a conflict between the old ways—the Elders—and the new ways—them?

"We want to do what's best for everyone," Ryn answered.

"We want to combine the technology from various settlements, to avoid causing additional problems," Eira said.

"And how will you do that?"

"First, by cleaning the toxins from the planet so we all have the chance to move about freely, and settle in new places," Ryn said.

"By removing the restrictions on education, so we have more people with a higher understanding of various sciences and arts," Aiden added.

Eira nodded. "And then we will work with other settlements to best assign resources and what to do with the new land. We can develop new technologies and use the resources we already have... such as the metals in Old Vancouver."

The Elders' expressions all grew more serious at the last suggestion. Aiden glanced around, trying to get a read on them. Suzanne looked as though she wasn't interested in hearing more, and Megan seemed as though she was struggling with it.

Lindsey cleared her throat noisily. Aiden took half a step forward, worried she was choking.

"Suzanne, tell these young ones about the teacher's plight," Lindsey said.

Sylvia handed her grandmother a cup with a straw, and Lindsey sipped at her water. Aiden monitored them, worried, while Suzanne spoke.

"It was only fifty years ago that New Vancouver nearly collapsed," Suzanne said. "We had developed a new fruit that could be grown on vines, but they weren't taking. There was no reason for them not to grow, but the vines were dying all over the city. The fields were producing next to nothing."

"What does this have to do with teachers?" Ryn asked, their brow furrowed.

Suzanne shook her head. "Patience."

Ryn grimaced and bowed. "I'm sorry for interrupting."

"We tried everything we could to increase the yield. We researched the old ways and realized that, even with our machines, we needed people in the fields daily. We needed people to go through the city and do the hard work required to keep our plants growing.

"But we Helians had spent too much of our lives sitting in class-rooms." Suzanne sighed heavily. "We lacked the strength necessary to do the physical labor. The robots were not enough, and we had illness after illness sweep through our ranks, making us even weaker. A group of adapted Subterraneans arrived as our salvation. Their strong bodies could do the physical toil that we could not.

Suzanne paused, then shook her head. "The rules for newcomers to need a certain number of hours came from the need to ensure that they did not grow weak as Helians did. We also have hours required for our citizens to work. Then came the teacher crisis, and we didn't have enough knowledgeable people to teach the new generations— and so we could not offer free education to everyone anymore.

"We thought it would be balanced out by newcomers with a high enough education from their previous homes. But that has not happened as quickly as we would like," Suzanne finished.

Aiden considered her words a moment, then faced her. "We didn't know that there had been that sort of difficulty. Thank you for telling us. I think one of the reasons it hasn't been filled as quickly as you thought is because education levels aren't taken into considera-tion with residency. Everyone has to work hours... but teaching posi-tions require a Helian teaching license, something that is difficult to get when you're working full hours already."

"Which is something that we've been debating for a few years now," Megan said as she shook her head. "But we wouldn't make a move, because we couldn't all agree on exactly what to do."

Aiden nodded slowly. It all made a lot more sense now, the rules. How many more were in place, ones that he didn't understand but were there because of something that New Vancouver had gone through?

"As for the resources of Old Vancouver," Lindsey said, drawing his attention back to her. "I lived in that city as a little girl. My grand-parents died in that city. What will you do when you harvest those metals and other resources?"

Aiden winced, though the question wasn't necessarily an accusation.

Eira answered slowly. "We can treat the remains we find with dignity and still salvage the resources we can find."

"There are no remains. That's the point," Lindsey said softly, her voice deepening with sadness. "The cloud... I won't go into the details. Only know that the bodies of the dead aren't in the city. They have become part of the city. Part of the metal you want to harvest."

Eira covered her mouth with her hands, tears in her eyes.

"Then that is something we will have to discuss and weigh," Ryn said slowly as they twisted their hands. "There's no easy answer when it comes to something like this. I would think it should be a city-wide vote, though. Perhaps more genealogical work needs to be done, to know exactly who in the city has ancestry in Old Vancouver."

Aiden kneeled beside Lindsey's chair and took her small hand in his. "I understand. You want to protect everyone. You have seen the problems the city has faced and put protections in place for those problems. But now we're facing new problems, and the old solutions aren't working."

"They aren't so big of problems as starvation, though," Lindsey told him.

Aiden laughed softly as he shook his head. "No. But they can't just be ignored because they don't have such high stakes, or they'll end up getting bigger, until only drastic action can save us."

"Drastic action... like an uprising that perhaps isn't as peaceful as yours was," Lindsey said, patting his cheek. Then a sadness came over her. What was she thinking about? She reached up to take her granddaughter's hand and patted it lightly. "New Vancouver cannot save the world."

Aiden bit his lip, hesitating. It was true. A single city couldn't be the salvation for everyone else. But... "Not everyone in the world needs to be saved. And perhaps it's time for New Vancouver to leave crisis mode and embrace the plenty that we have."

"There are so many settlements isolated within themselves," Ryn added. "The larger world is at risk. Eira told us about the old days, when humans were in isolated communities, when they didn't think of themselves as human but as members of their group and different from other groups. If we let that happen again, then just like those old days, conflict will emerge."

"New Vancouver is not offering a way for people to integrate into a new culture while holding respect to where they came from," Eira added. "We need unity. You are all quite right. But we need unity that embraces our differences, and understands that maybe we're not all that different after all."

Aiden squeezed Lindsey's hand softly. "We as the New Council don't want to replace the Elder Council. We want to work with you, to understand the past and the trauma that brought you here."

"It's the only way." Ryn came to stand next to him and rested a hand on his shoulder.

Eira came to his other side. "So. What do you say? Will you accept that change is needed?"

Lindsey smiled.

19

ECHOES TO ANTHEMS

"YOU'RE RIGHT," Lindsey said, and Aiden's breath burst out of him. Relief washed through his body so strongly he nearly sagged. Linsey patted his cheek and nodded, almost to herself. "I will release a statement of my own, with or without the other Elders on my side. I've never thought much about this 'all speak with the same voice' crock of nonsense, anyway."

"Mother," Megan said, groaning. "We agreed—"

Lindsey shook her head. "You agreed. You all thought I was asleep, but I was listening. Besides, I'm technically not a part of the Elder Council, seeing as I haven't been voted in for years."

"The silence has been the worst part," Ryn told Morgan, then turned to Suzanne, who frowned. "Honestly, it was driving us all crazy. A statement will only help people to feel you're actually doing something."

Suzanne scowled, but nodded. "Very well. Now. We should get started, then. What will be our first order of business?"

AIDEN CLUTCHED HIS PALMHELD, his eyes skimming over the notes written there. It was the first official conference with both the Elder Council and the New Council together. Cameras were set up, filming them all. He was glad that he would not have to talk first.

He was surprised at how difficult it was to talk in front of all these people. He glanced up from his palmheld, swallowed, and sought the familiar faces in the crowd. His shoulders relaxed when he found Shuang, who held both her thumbs up to him.

He grinned back. The pressure in his chest released as he saw Mama Bunting, Yaella, and Ayasha standing next to Shuang.

Even though he, Eira, and Ryn no longer worked at the café, they stopped by often to see how things were going. A new group of Subterrans had replaced the three of them and things were moving smoothly at the café. The three of them had also gotten a new apartment that they shared, but kept in contact with the lovely couple that had helped them out so much when they first arrived.

Elder Sylvia stepped up to the podium. "Hello. We are very pleased to announce today that we announce the formal inauguration of the New Council. We of the Elders recognize how difficult it has been for years now, and we are grateful for the New Council for having the wisdom to step in when we were blinded by the past.

"We cannot express the sorrow we felt as we realized that the very things we thought were protecting our city were hurting the people here. We now vow for this to change, and we look forward to working with the new generations to make the future.

"With that said," Sylvia continued, her voice strong and melodious as she smiled at the gathered crowd, "we are pleased to announce that there will be an election held for the Elder Council next year. It is vital that all voices be heard, and so we are opening these elections up for not only citizens but also residents who have been in the city ten years or more to run for a place on the Council.

"The elections for the New Council will be held the year after. Just as the Elder Council has a minimum age requirement for those who can sit on it, the New Council will have a maximum age requirement. That way, we ensure we don't end up with two Elder Councils," Sylvia said with a laugh.

Applause answered her words. Aiden clapped as well. His stomach tightened—he was up next.

"The New Council has decided on three speakers to address you now," Sylvia said. "It is my pleasure to hand the podium over to Mr. Aiden."

He swallowed, his mouth suddenly dry. The campaigning had been nothing compared to this—probably because it happened so quickly he hadn't had the chance to really think things through. Now, though, he'd known this was coming for a few weeks. That time had allowed him to think through everything that could go wrong.

Well, no more time for thinking. He stepped up to the podium. "Thank you, Elder Sylvia."

He swallowed as he looked out over the crowd again, then focused in on Shuang again. She was grinning at him and he grinned back.

"Through the help with various Subterran people, we've been in contact with over twenty Subterran fallout shelters which originated from Vancouver. We have begun working with them to retrofit the terraforming caches left across the world, so that when the pollutants are collected out of land and water, they can be broken down.

"We are still in the building stage, but we hope that not only can we prevent these pollutants from poisoning the earth again, but actually rebuilt into useful compounds. So far we have been able to create not only fresh water, but some preliminary metals as well."

Applause answered. It was a tremendous breakthrough, to actually create the resources they needed by changing the composition of the molecules and atoms of the pollution.

"There is still much work to be done," he continued once the crowd had quieted down. "We must make sure that doing this won't cause more harm than good. We are also looking into alternative resources, so that we don't have to use metal in our construction.

"As we look forward, we must be certain that we think about

what we can do for this world. It will take a long time to restore the planet to the green paradise, full of animals and beautiful things, that it once was. Perhaps it's not possible." Aiden glanced at his palmheld again, his eyes skimming the last notes he put down. He'd covered everything. "However, we will do our best to create a land that has space for us all.

He took a deep breath and finished, "Now I would like to turn the podium over to my colleague, Miss Eira."

Eira nodded her thanks to Aiden and lightly squeezed his hand as they passed one another. Her hands shook slightly, but she wasn't sure if the butterflies in her stomach were more nerves or excitement. She stepped up to the podium.

"Many of you by now have heard of Fata Morgana's caches of seeds and animal DNA. The Aerians have been growing new seeds for decades now, and releasing those seeds in waves over the land, hoping for the plants to filter out the toxins from the land. Now, with the new terraforming programs, these seed releases will be put on hold for five years.

"However, we have arranged with Fata Morgana to start an intensive restoration process in the lands around New Vancouver. We will establish various nurseries for the animals throughout the Cascade Mountains. We will keep these new populations well-guarded in limited spaces to observe how they do in the forests. As the terraforming spreads, so too will the restorative processes.

Eira grinned, pressing both of her hands on the podium. Her heart skipped with excitement as she thought of the many animals that she used to see on her TV screen. "We hope to restore ecosystems once the terraforming is complete, but will need many volunteers to raise the animals and study old texts so we can understand behavior and other needs."

There was a round of clapping in answer to her words. Eira let it die down before she continued. This was the most important part.

"We have also discussed what to do with the new fauna that has arisen to fill the niches left by extinct animals. The wolf rats are something we are all familiar with. In the old days, humans led to the extinction of hundreds of species. We have decided that it's not right for us to eliminate these new species for the sake of the old ones. Therefore, as part of the program, we will need research done into the animals on the planet right now. We will work to adapt the old species with the new ones, so that there is space for both in this world."

She took a moment to gauge her reaction. There were a few confused faces in the crowd. Others nodded their agreement, while one or two scowled. She understood.

It was highly likely that the wolf rats weren't a natural creature. They could prove to be a huge detriment to their attempts to repopulate the planet with creatures like deer and true wolves. But they had carved out a place here in the world, and it seemed wrong to wipe them out for the sake of what once was, rather than seeking more knowledge as to what role they actually filled.

"More news of this program will be delivered as we make progress," Eira finished. "Now I'd like to turn the time over to Mx. Ryn."

Ryn confidently took the podium. "We have established contact with the Aquatics and have already started cleansing the oceans. Now, you are all aware of the dangers this poses, as we don't yet have a reliable means to dissipate the collected toxins. However, given the vastness of the ocean and how vital it is to every other aspect of life on Earth, we have concluded that there is no time to waste.

"Currently, we are working with the Aquatics to create stores of the solidified toxins, to keep it out of the way until we're able to use the Subterran technology to rewrite it at a molecular level. In exchange for this, the Aquatics are sending teachers to New Vancouver. We are extremely pleased to announce that from this day onward, all education will be free for all citizens and residents of the city."

Ryn sipped on some water. Eira looked out over the crowd, beaming when she saw the familiar faces of the friends she'd made along the way. There were others, too, people grinning up at them, others with expressions of concentration.

Even Mr. Julian, the vendor who had been so mean to the three of them, was in attendance. His face was twisted, but Eira didn't know if he was upset or thoughtful. Not everyone in the city was happy for these developments, but then, with a population this size, it would never be possible for everyone to get exactly what they wanted.

She hoped, though, that this would bring about the most good to the most people... and that none of their new policies would cause harm to even a fraction of the population.

"Everything that happened these last few months could have torn us apart," Ryn said, their voice strong. "But thanks to the dedication and determination of everyone in this city, we have been able to find what matters most. Thank you, all of you. New Vancouver will serve as a beacon of hope across the world."

The audience burst into clapping. Eira joined with them. The future would be hard, but it would be bright. She was certain of it.

20
LEGACY'S RHYTHM

SYLVIA PULLS a blanket over Lindsey's knees, tucking it around her. There's concern in her granddaughter's face, so Lindsey takes her hand and pats it.

"I'm quite alright. Why don't you go get me some of that ginger punch?" she says with a smile.

Sylvia kisses her cheek and makes sure the brakes are on the wheelchair before she heads off. Lindsey relaxes back into her chair, her hands folded over her lap. She closes her eyes, listening to the music that comes from the large speakers. It's a beautiful melody, reminding her of the days of her childhood, dancing with her parents in the bunker.

Oh, there has been so much sorrow over these last hundred years. But there has been so much joy as well.

A smile passes over her lips. She fought so hard to make a better future for her children, her grandchildren, her great-grandchildren, and great-great-grandchildren.

Now she can see that she was successful. Everything she had hoped New Vancouver would be had come to fruition. They would never go hungry again. They would never suffer from wondering if they had space for a new generation. They would never fear the utter collapse of everything and the death of the planet.

She opens her eyes and seeks the three teenagers. Ryn dances with their Aquatic friend, Aalton, who is newly arrived to the city as part of an ambassadorial program.

Ryn looks so much like Paula. The same inky-black hair, the same vibrant, dark skin. Eyes, ears, the shape of their mouth; everything is exactly like Lindsey's old friend.

Lindsey idly thinks about the painting she'd made for her friend when Paula had sought out other settlements. She had painted Paula on an iceberg, surrounded by the flickering lightning. Paula loved thunderstorms.

Sylvia returns with ginger punch. Lindsey drinks through a straw, holding the cup with both hands. Watching Ryn dance, she thinks she finally knows what happened with Paula. It would be nice to take a DNA sample to confirm Ryn is her descendant, but ultimately, it's unnecessary. Ryn is here, which means Paula was successful.

"It's a beautiful party, isn't it?" Sylvia says as she sits next to Lindsey.

"It most certainly is. Today should be a yearly celebration, the day that New Vancouver officially opened its doors to integrating all settlements," Lindsey agrees, bobbing her head in time with the music.

It's called 'New' Vancouver for a reason. If they had remained mired in the past, how could they be new?

The city had led the way; more and more settlements were announcing their presence now, and they were all working together, uniting to build a collective future of bounty and cooperation.

Eira is nearby to Ryn, with her sister and young nephew. They're talking animatedly, their volume just loud enough that Lindsey can catch the occasional snippet of conversation. They also keep hugging one another.

"It must be a tremendous relief, knowing they can come to and from Fata Morgana with our helicopters," Lindsey says.

"What was that?" Sylvia leans in closer.

Lindsey laughs. "The music is wonderful."

"Oh, it is. And we'll be having firelights soon," Sylvia says.

Lindsey nods and lowers her drink. "Go grab me a couple of those little cupcakes, will you? Thank you, dear."

Sylvia leaves again, and Lindsey leans a little closer to Eira and her sister. One of the best things about being so old is being able to eavesdrop.

"I'm so proud of you," Eira's sister says. "We all are. When we saw you had been elected to the New Council, you can't imagine our shock. Then when we learned what you've accomplished here... You really are amazing, Eira."

"Oh, I didn't do anything on my own," Eira answers, her bluish skin darkening with a blush.

Her sister grins. "And thanks to you, my husband and I have joined the animal program. He's wanted to for so long but didn't want to leave the city. Now we can go back and forth and there's no reason not to. I've gotten a contract to build up the living quarters for the village, to hold the increased numbers."

"I know," Eira says, laughing. "It was part of the proposal sent to the council to ask for New Vancouver to supply the village with food for both humans and animals. You can't say anything because we haven't given an official answer yet, but we're going to say yes. Not only that, but the first location for the new terraforming is in the valleys to the east of the village, to help with developing their own food production."

Lindsey nods, satisfied with what she's heard. She's been a little too ill to attend meetings lately but put in her wishes so they'd be known.

She unlocks the brakes of her wheelchair and navigates it through the dancers. Several of them bow in respect and she offers the proper words. Finally, she gets to the other side of the room where Aiden is. Since these three teens are the ones that caused everything to blossom, she's most eager to find where they are during this celebration.

She settles close by, where Aiden sits with his friends Pat and Shuang. The two girls are having an arm-wrestling contest while Aiden eggs them both on. They look like they're having a great time.

Ever the observant one, Aiden catches sight of her. He excuses himself from his friends and comes over.

"Eldest Lindsey," he says, bowing to her.

"Ugh, none of that formality," Lindsey answers, waving her hand. "Just Lindsey. Calling me 'Eldest' makes me think that I'm a dragon rider."

She chuckles at the confusion in his face. Not about to explain her little joke. She gestures to the seat next to her and invites him to sit. He does so, looking over the celebration with a thoughtful expression. There are deep words in his eyes and Lindsey watches him, waiting for him to speak.

"Do you think it will work?" he finally asks.

"What is that? There are many things that we hope will work, Aiden. Be more specific."

Aiden smiles and shakes his head. "Oh, I think you understand what I mean. Integrating our different societies. Using the terraforming equipment to restore the planet. I'm afraid that we're trying to go too big all at once and it will collapse."

Lindsey holds her hand out to him, and he takes it. "Listen to me, Aiden. There is always the risk of collapse. That is why watchers like you and I are so important. That's your job, you know. To watch how things go and to see when there are weak spots. Eira is the dreamer. Ryn is the pusher. You are the watcher. You all have your parts in this future."

Aiden hums as he frowns. His head cocks to one side as he works through her words. "You mean we each bring our own strengths to the table and must work together?"

"Exactly. And your part is to worry about it collapsing, and to pull back when things are moving a little too fast. You have a lot of learning, but you'll get there."

Sylvia sees them and approaches, but Lindsey holds up a hand. Sylvia nods and turns to Suzanne, who stands nearby, and begins talking with her.

Lindsey takes Aiden's hand in hers and gives it a grandmotherly squeeze.

"I'm very grateful that you three took up the mantel. You're smart kids. Full of compassion and hope, just what we need. You've opened a lot of old eyes." She smiles as she gazes over the other Elders. "You're exactly what we needed, exactly when we needed you."

Aiden blushes. "You sound surprised that we could do it."

"Of course I am! It's difficult to get people to acknowledge what needs to be changed, and you managed." She laughs and drinks some more punch. "Things have changed so much since I was your age. I've pushed through a lot, but even when I was sixteen I wouldn't have been able to do it."

She pauses as a peculiar image flashes before her eyes. Suddenly, she is not sitting in the Council Building in New Vancouver, but deep beneath the surface. She's no longer an old woman, but a young girl.

She sees herself, hands clasped in her parent's hands, as the three of them dance in a circle. They laugh and sing as the lights sway overhead. Then the scene changes once more, and it's her wedding day. Her arms are around her husband as they turn on the spot, gazing at once another with loving eyes. One by one, each of her children joins them, then grows.

The family keeps getting bigger. First her children's spouses step into the dance, then the grandchildren. It's a beautiful sight. Even when her eyes fill with tears at the beauty of it, she sees is all clearly. Great-grandchildren grow swiftly and are joined by the littlest babies, her great-great grandchildren.

They will know a better life. They will have a glorious future.

Lindsey is certain that she can see even more. Generations that have not yet been born, stretching on and on on the horizon. Oh, they'll have their struggles, no doubt. But it's good to know that her pain, her work, was not in vain. Perhaps she won't be able to see the replenished world, but it will come.

And that is enough. Knowing that her work did something is enough.

"Are you alright?" Aiden asks in worry as Lindsey wipes a tear from her eye.

"Oh, yes. I'm quite alright. Just getting a little tired." She pats his hand. "I hope that even with your responsibilities with the council, you will continue your studies. You're a smart boy and deserve time to pursue your own passions."

Aiden grins at her. "Oh, you can be certain of it. I've been carving time out every week so that I can finish the schooling I'd have in Bunk 37."

"Good."

"I think that might be my next goal, to bring in some sort of a minimum standard that people should be allowed to meet before too much is required of them. I'm not sure how it will work, though. Some people might not want that intensity."

"Perhaps then your challenge is not to establish a minimum, but to establish accessibility."

Aiden nods, his eyes lighting up. "Thank you. That's exactly what I need to do."

Lindsey releases his hand and slumps a little lower in her chair. She's growing more tired, although this is to be expected at her age. She hums along to the beat of the music, considering what advice she would give her younger self if she could.

"It won't be easy, you know," she says to Aiden, tapping her toes as she does so.

"What was that?" he asks, leaning in to hear her better.

She clears her throat and speaks a little louder. "You and your friends have a long road ahead of yourselves. There will be upsets. Problems you can't even imagine yet. You are going to find yourselves on opposite sides with multiple issues."

"Oh." Aiden's brow furrows. It's clear he's confused about why she's bringing this up now of all times.

Lindsey has to smile to herself. It must seem rather random to him. But what was the point of being old if you couldn't have a little fun with it every once in a while? He didn't need to understand why she was bringing this up, only that she was talking of it.

"My friend Paula and I had some terrible fights over what we thought we should do," she continues, her eyes on Ryn once more. "But even when we weren't certain our friendship would survive, we knew we were both wanting the same goal. A better future. So we always came back to each other."

Aiden nods, wearing that thoughtful expression.

"So long as you and your friends continue to embrace your core values, the world will be a better place than it once was," Lindsey tells him. Then she adds, "Paula built herself a submarine to search the oceans. She was certain that there were settlements that had fled below the water. Your friend Ryn looks exactly like her."

"Do they?" Aiden asked in surprise. "Ryn's parents died in an accident when they were only a few weeks old... but your friend would be too old to be their mother."

Lindsey laughs. "I never said Paula was their mother, Aiden. I said they look like her."

Eira joins Ryn and the two of them look around. They spy Aiden and wave him over. He hesitates and Lindsey pats his shoulder.

"Go on."

He grins at her and heads over to his friends. Lindsey folds her hands in her lap as Sylvia comes over. She wheels Lindsey over to the window, where the firelights are lighting the sky. Hundreds of glowing insects are released, forming a brilliant display that swoops overhead. It's so beautiful, Lindsey sighs.

She's unable to see the definition she once did, but she thinks things are getting clearer every day.

"Go ahead back to the party, Sylvia," Lindsey says. "I'm just going to have a rest."

She smiles as she closes her eyes to sleep.

EPILOGUE

RYN

I step through the barrier to Aquata, the crystal-clear water rolling off my protective suit as I transition from water to air. The visiting quarters for land-dwellers have just been finished, meaning this is my first visit to the city. After I stepped down from the council last year, I was asked to be an ambassador. How could I refuse?

"Aalton," I greet my old friend with a hug.

"Happy birthday!" he exclaims.

Heat rushes to my cheeks, and I step back, grinning at him. "Come on! I'm meant to be an official ambassador. You need to be more formal than that."

Aalton shakes his head. "No way. You're my best friend, Ryn. I'm not going to act all stuffy until I absolutely have to. Besides, today's the big 3-o! I've been planning the party all week."

I grin at him, warmth blossoming in my chest. Ah, there's nothing quite like coming home. It's strange to me I have never been to the city before, and yet it feels as much like home as New Vancouver does. Probably because of the friends I still have here.

"Do you want to settle in first or go to the nurseries?" he asks me.

My eyes light up. "Nurseries, please!"

He laughs and guides me through the corridors. Even though this part of the city is air-based, I still need to wear my protective gear, seeing as we're so far under the water. The pressure of the ocean creatures has a different pressure in the air itself, which would influence me if I don't wear the suit. Luckily, it protects me perfectly.

Aalton leads me to the nurseries, which are giant pods where various species are being raised. The fishes are in other sections of Aquata, but here they're raising the mammals. Sea lions, seals, dolphins, and other aquatic or semi-aquatic air-breathers. A small pack of otters comes scurrying over to the large windows when they see us.

"They're getting so big," I say in surprise.

The last I saw them, it was a small, artificial womb where the embryos were being developed. That was before they were sent down here. They should be where the fishes are also being bred and raised, seeing how they will be fishers once they're released.

Above the ocean, our animal programs are focused on the land creatures. They're doing well also, although I don't visit those programs myself.

"They're almost old enough to be transferred to the surface," Aalton tells me, beaming. "Although they haven't figured out how to catch fish for themselves just yet. But that's why the safety tanks are being built, isn't it?"

I nod. "They're going well, too, although perhaps not as quickly as we wanted. But I have every confidence in our teams."

"Good. I'm looking forward to seeing it all in action. The schools of salmon we released are doing so well, I'm eager to build up the predator populations as well."

"Me, too." I wiggle my fingers in front of the otters and they follow along with their chubby little bodies. It makes me laugh.

We continue on, with Aalton explaining the successes and failures they'd had so far. We were all eager for whales to be reintroduced, but thus far it had been impossible to recreate their migration patterns. The oceans have been thoroughly scrubbed free of pollutants, but the ice at either pole still holds onto toxins which caused some concern.

"Shuang has a few new ideas of how to deal with the ice," I tell Aalton after we're done the tour. "I think she's brilliant. I'm sure that it'll work. We just have to be careful about not disrupting too much of the ice caps all at once."

Aalton slings an arm around my shoulders. "And none of this would have been possible without the cooperation of New Vancouver. For that matter, it never would have happened if you hadn't gone to the surface."

I put my arm around him as well as we head toward the Ambassador's quarters. After over a decade of serving on the New Council, I can hardly believe the amount of work we've accomplished.

I've changed and grown so much. I hardly recognize the child I used to be. "I wouldn't have, if the Dome hadn't failed. What seemed like the worst day of my life at the time ended up changing everything for the better."

"I was afraid I'd never see you again." Aalton lets out a shuddering breath.

Cupping his face, I turn him to me. "But you have. We're both here, we're both happy and healthy. We're both working hard for the things that we love."

He smiles with his eyes at me.

We get to my quarters. Technology from Fata Morgana has been used to make these rooms comfortable and stable without the protective suit, so I change into something more casual. I'll be going to see the Aquata councils tomorrow. Today, my birthday, is all about spending time with my friends.

"Irta is coming by later," Aalton tells me. "Valdimar, too. They both wanted me to make sure you know they were going to visit."

"I'm looking forward to seeing them."

"Ryn, did you ever figure out where that painting came from? The one that showed you on the ice?" Aalton asks.

I take a moment to remember what he's talking about. I haven't thought about that painting in a very long time. I hum in thought, considering the question.

"I have theories, but that's all. You've seen pictures of my great-great-grandmother, Paula?" I prompt.

Aalton nods.

"She came from the surface, and from the records I've seen, she stayed in that section of the Dome when she was brought in after her submarine was destroyed," I say, wrapping my hands around my knees. "Since I look so much like her, I think it must be a painting of her, one that she brought with her. But I'll never have proof."

"I always thought it was someone from the past who got a glimpse of the future and put that painting there to make sure that you'd head to the surface. Because, after all, all of this is because of you."

I roll my eyes, though I think the sentiment is sweet. "I don't think so. Besides, it's not all because of me. There have been too many people involved for me to take credit for it."

Aalton grins at me.

I squint suspiciously. "What?"

"I'm just thinking about everything. That painting really did kick-start it all. I wish I could thank the artist. And yeah, there have been a lot of others involved, but you can't discount what you've done." Aalton shakes his head with a laugh. "That's all. Just that so much has changed... all for the better."

"Thanks."

I lean back in my chair as I consider it. It hasn't been a smooth road. There were plenty of hiccups along the way. More than once, I wondered if I was still suited for it. More than once, I wanted to give up.

Now, though, I've seen the results of my work. I'm so grateful to everyone who supported me to get to this point. And I'm looking forward to everything that will happen next. New Vancouver really is the beacon I wanted it to be.

A beacon of hope, prosperity—and regrowth.

EIRA

I rub the belly of the fawn as she walks on unsteady legs. She's only a few hours old, her mother nearby munching on the pellets that have been left out for her. The ultrasound imager in my palm transmits an image to the screen I'm looking in. With a sigh of relief, I confirm that the little fawn is perfectly healthy.

We've been worried about this little one since her mother had gotten badly injured while pregnant. It looks like there was no lasting damage, though. I smile as I put away the equipment.

If you told me ten years ago that I'd be a veterinarian, I wouldn't have believed you. I wanted to stay working with Mama Bunting. But then I visited the village more and more often, so I could see Elzi, her husband, and their kids. I fell in love with the deer and other animals that the village was raising.

My youngest nephew, Lyr, takes the equipment from me so I can climb over the stall door. My oxygen mask catches, but I gently detangle it and put it back on. Up here at the peak of the mountain, the air is still too thin for me to breathe comfortably. As it turns out, I have a lung condition that makes me more suspectible to thin air than even Helians, Subterraneans and Aquatics.

"Is she going to be okay?" Lyr asks, reaching through the stall bars to pat the fawn's head.

"She sure is," I say.

He grins. He's almost eleven now and his baby face is thinning out. He'll be a teenager soon. "Good! Because she's supposed to be one of the initial deer taken to the Yukon. Mama and Papa say we're going to go, too, just as soon as the ice terraformers are up and running."

I ruffle his hair. "And here I thought you were going to be a student at my veterinarian college. We need experienced students like you."

I wink at him to show I'm kidding. I have been working like crazy to restore the last husbandry knowledge, but it's been slow going. The school I hope to establish will not only teach the practicality of caring for animals but also include a great deal of research so we don't have to learn only by trial and error.

"I'll come back for veterinarian school," Lyr tells me as we head out of the barn. A chill wind whips across the bald head of the mountain.

We pause in the cold air as the burgeoning wolf pack howls. The deer programs have been extremely successful—a little too successful, as they're overpopulating the area. We need some predators to cull them so we don't have to do it ourselves.

"Thank you, Aunt Eira," Lyr says, turning to me.

I laugh. "For what?"

"For everything you've done. In class yesterday, we were learning about the formation of the New Council in New Vancouver. I never knew you were part of it." He throws his arms around me tightly. "Teacher says that the village would have failed if it weren't for the New Council's work. So thank you."

A lump rises in my throat. I decided years ago I would not be a mother myself, but I still love spending time with kids. Especially my own nibblings. I hug Lyr back, so grateful.

Everything I've done, it's for him and the others of his generation. Even before I realized that's why I was doing it, my focus was so much on them. It's been a long road, but I'm so very grateful for everything that brought me here.

Lyr releases me and we head to his home. It's toasty warm inside and I remove my mask. Elzi has a special oxygen machine that allows the entire building to keep me breathing properly that she uses while I visit, though it's uncomfortable for her.

None of her children have had to go through the painful adaptations she and I went through, though, and they don't even notice the difference.

"Eira, did you complete your examination?" Elzi asks. Her anxious eyes tell me she's been worried about the fawn as well.

"Perfectly healthy."

Elzi lets out a whoop and punches the air. She laughs as Lyr dances over to her and they hug each other. Supper is on the table, growing cold, so I sit up and start dishing myself up some food. Everyone else has already eaten—I ended up working with the animals much later than I anticipated.

"Run along and get ready for bed," Elzi tells Lyr.

He nods and trots off.

Elzi slips into the chair next to mine and heaves out a long sigh. "Oh, Eira. I'm so happy that things have worked out. I've been so worried about that doe and her fawn. I know that they're not vital for the project but every creature is important."

"I know. It's been a lot of hard work. Just keeping the genetics clear is a massive project in of itself." I eat my mashed potatoes, a dish that I have grown extremely fond of over the years.

Elzi rests her chin in her hand. "Did you hear about the new rules being implemented in Fata Morgana?"

"No."

"Since the radiation shielding technology from Subterran settlements is working the way they want it to, adaptations on infants and toddlers have been halted. There are more and more spaces that are being supplemented with oxygen."

I lower my spoon, eyes wide. "Enough that children don't need to go through the adaptations?"

Elzi beams and nods. "More research is being done, but it seems like it might be possible to delay the adaptations until the children are old enough to decide for themselves, rather than being necessary for survival."

"That's amazing!"

Over the last ten years, it was discovered that whatever was in me, Ryn, and Aiden that prevented the adaptations from being effective in us wasn't unique. One out of every thousand children can't be surgically adapted.

Hearing the news that Fata Morgana is adapting itself to be a suitable environment, rather than putting the children through these adaptations, fills me with hope.

"Perhaps some day I'll be able to walk through the streets without my mask," I say, fingering the oxygen mask still on my belt. It's a necessary tool, but I long to be able to exist in my old home without it. If only to visit my family, still there.

"You will," Elzi says. She pats my arm. "I'm certain of it."

I grin at her and resume eating. Tomorrow, I will return to New Vancouver but this is excellent news to take back. I just know that my friends will be just as excited to hear about it.

AIDEN

I lock the door and switch the sign from 'open' to 'closed' before I grab the broom. It's been a busy day, and I stopped by Mama Bunting's café at this time on purpose. Her dark hair has streaks of gray in it and she's not moving as quickly as she once did. That smile she gives me is as youthful as it was ten years ago, though.

"Councilor Aiden, you don't have to do that," she tells me, reaching for the broom.

I pull it away, out of her reach, and shake my head. "I told you long ago there was nothing I could do to repay your kindness, but I'll continue to try. Besides, I enjoy cleaning. It brings back a lot of wonderful memories."

Mama Bunting shakes her head at me, but goes behind the counter to clean it off. I watch her, debating whether I should tell her to go rest. She's been sick these last couple of weeks, but she hates to sit still.

It's strange to me, the arc that comes with growing older. I've been gaining more and more experience and understanding, but eventually there will be the younger generations telling me to go take a rest and not work so hard, either.

I hope that's not for many years yet, though. I'm only twenty-seven; though I remember at seventeen, this age seemed impossibly old.

There's a tinkling noise in the back, indicating that door has been opened. Ryn and Eira step through to the front.

"Oh, my dears!" Mama Buntings rushes over to hug the two newcomers. "I didn't think either of you were returning until tomorrow!"

Ryn laughs. "The trip from the shoreline back to New Vancouver was shorter than anticipated. The new walking legs are fast!"

"I arrived back this morning. I just had a lot of work to finish up before I could pop over," Eira says apologetically.

Mama Bunting clasps her hands together. "I have an ice-cream cake in the freezer. Let me get it."

She skips off, looking lighter. Eira picks up cleaning where she left off while Ryn lifts the chairs over the tables, just like they used to. The three of them work companionably. Though Mama Bunting always has willing workers, it's nice sometimes to go back to the first job they had here in New Vancouver.

"How did your trips go?" I ask after some time.

"Wonderful," Ryn answered. "Aquata has made huge leaps forward. I'll have plenty to report to the Councils tomorrow."

Eira nods. "I will as well. I have a few tweaks to the proposal I want to include. But I had a great visit with my family. How about you? Have you and Shuang contacted those fallout shelters over the seas?"

"We contacted ten of them. All thought that the world above here was still poison, and we'll be sending people to explain our mission soon. We're still deciding if the airplanes are ready for overseas travel yet."

It's been years since we worked here, but we quickly get through all the chores. Mama Bunting returns with the cake, which she sets on a table. The four of us sit down and hear all about the new crop of workers. Eira shows us pictures she received from her family, images of the planet captured from Fata Morgana.

In the past ten years, the green spaces have blossomed once more. It's a beautiful sight which fills me with joy.

"These are my favorites," Eira says as she gets to a handful of new ones. "They're images that have been zoomed in to check on species diversity. Look at all the colors!"

Mama Bunting claps her hands, her eyes lighting up.

The first image is of a large meadow full of flowers. The blossoms are of every color imaginable, and with a shock of delight, I see dozens of little insects buzzing about. Tears fill in my eyes. These are the delicate winged species—butterflies, bees, and the like—that had all been wiped out by the cloud.

"I'm certain we'll start seeing more animals take over these habitats soon," Eira says. "The mouse and vole program has been working wonderfully. The hawks, owls, and eagles follow them wherever they go. It's amazing, isn't it? The way the natural world comes together?"

"It really is," I say.

Mama Bunting points at the next picture, a closeup of a daisy. "Can I have a copy of that to hang on my wall?"

Eira nods. "Of course."

"I'm going to have to bring a potted plant down to Aalton the next time I visit him," Ryn says musingly. They've finished their slice of cake and lean on their elbows. "This is amazing, Eira. Fata Morgana has done so much good work."

We keep looking at pictures and discussing everything that happened on our recent trips until Mama Bunting starts to yawn and nod off. Then, we make our excuses so as not to make her feel bad and say goodnight.

"Visit again when you're able," she says.

"We will," I promise as I kiss her cheek.

It's a chilly dusk as we head back through the familiar trails. We all live in the same building, though we haven't shared an apartment in many years. I breathe in the clear air, lifting my face toward the sky.

As we pass through the market district, the vendors are all closing up their shops. Mr. Julian waves to us, a smile breaking over his face. Though he once was what I considered being the most awful person in the city, things have changed since then.

Not that it hadn't taken a long time.

"Councillor Aiden! Miss Eira. Mx. Ryn," Julian calls, waving us over. "I have some extra cakes. Would you like to take them home?"

"Thank you," I say, accepting the gift, as I have for years now. It's just more proof of how the city has come together and changed even the hardest of hearts.

We take a break in a small park to eat our fluffy cakes. Stars shine overhead and Eira turns her face to the sky.

"Remember how we all met? Three lost kids, afraid and alone. But we found each other in this city."

I nod my agreement. "I'd never met anyone who was more like me than you two. Even though we came from such different backgrounds, I knew I found lifelong friends the moment we met."

Ryn laughs. "Same! Funny thing, isn't it? Life."

"Yeah," Eira says.

I smile. Funny, yes. But life is also good. "To us," I say on impulse, raising my cake to the sky. "May we always be changing for the better."

"Hear, hear!" my friends cry, lifting their cakes.

Then we eat beneath the twinkling stars. All is bright in the world.

The End

Did you enjoy *Utopia?*

Please consider rating or reviewing it on Goodreads, Bookbub, or your favorite platform.

Reviews help me reach new readers.

Help me decide which story to write next by reading *What Happens Next?*

Join my newsletter for writing updates, sneak peaks, review copies, sales, and giveaways! www.mhlebeault.com

www.ingramcontent.com/pod-product-compliance
Lightning Source LLC
Chambersburg PA
CBHW031959240626
47153CB00003B/1042